Books by Jon Keys

Single Titles

Tackling the Subject

Tackling the Subject

ISBN # 978-1-78686-197-9

©Copyright Jon Keys 2017

Cover Art by Posh Gosh ©Copyright 2017

Interior text design by Claire Siemaszkiewicz

Pride Publishing

Published in 2017 by Pride Publishing, Think Tank, Ruston Way, Lincoln, LN6 7FL, United Kingdom.

Pride Publishing is a subsidiary of Totally Entwined Group Limited.

TACKLING THE SUBJECT

JON KEYS

Chapter One

A shaft of light landed on the thick red hair covering Sam's forearm. He shifted a little deeper into the tomb-quiet, cavernous room. The rows and rows of books in their order and symmetry had always comforted him—just like writing code for new software, which he was kick ass at doing. There should be logic to biology, too. It might not be obvious, but somewhere in all that squishiness it had order. Sam liked things that had order.

He glanced at the screen of his computer. No new mail. Their appointment was at three. Not three-o-five. Sam was already angry that he'd had to ask for a tutor. Well, really more embarrassed that some whiz kid had to explain the confusing field of biology. Sam resented the hell out of it. *Mutation?* Computers didn't mutate. Code didn't mutate. It was driving him crazy.

He glanced at his watch again. Two more minutes. He sighed and reminded himself that he had to pass this class. It was one of those courses he'd had to take outside his major. *If I wanted to know about meiosis and mitosis, then I'd take the class on my own. But the university thinks I need to be educated about crap I don't care about.*

The air conditioner came on and a shaft of cool air blew across him. It carried an almost antiseptic tang along with the faint musty scent of books printed before his grandparents' time. He glanced at the screen on his watch. *Another minute and he'll be late. It figures.*

Sam stretched his long legs, letting his flip-flops dangle from his bare toes. He realized someone had invaded his part of the library's fifth floor. His frown deepened when he recognized it was one of the brainless hulks from the football team. Sam tensed as the lumbering brute moved closer. *Go away. Go back to your cave and leave normal people alone.*

His discomfort level grew as the guy walked toward him. *Short dark hair, western shirt, jeans and boots. Well, he's at the right university.* Their distance narrowed and Sam dropped his gaze in the hope he would pass without stopping. His nervousness built until, by the time they were side by side, there was a slight tremble going through his body and bile in his mouth. Triggers from years past fired like a cheap six-gun. He tensed even further when the guy stopped beside him. Sam was angry and his appraisal turned into a glare he shot at the lummox. But before he said anything, he heard.

"Are you Samuel Doherty?"

At first, it startled Sam that the guy had his name. But his rancor flared when he realized the man was reading it from a card and held a copy of his biology textbook under one arm. *This is my tutor? It's bad enough I need help at all. This makes it insulting.* He looked up and scowled. "Yes, I'm Sam."

"Cool. I'm Gordy, your biology tutor."

Sam sat stunned, staring in disbelief at the person they'd sent. Without considering the consequences, he blurted out. "Wasn't there anyone else?"

Gordy lifted an eyebrow and gave him a quiet expression of disapproval. "I aced the class you're failing, so I'm quite capable of helping you. But it's up to you if you want my assistance or not."

Sam sat without moving then realized the jock — *What's his name? Gordy?* — was still waiting for an answer. Just getting help from one of the university jock squad had his muscles taut with anger and distaste. But the midterm was coming, and he had to pass this class. If this was who the Help Center had assigned him, then he was capable of helping Sam. But with feelings approaching hatred, Sam didn't understand how he would get the assistance he needed from Gordy. *It had to be a damn football player?*

"I can go if you want. I had to rearrange everything to meet with you today, so…" Gordy said.

Sam swallowed hard. *I have to suppress my feelings. I don't know him. He might be a good guy. I suppose that's possible. That's one of the goals from the therapist. That I shouldn't paint everyone with the same broad strokes.* Gordy frowned and turned to go, leaving Sam to his private corner.

"Hang on. Yeah, I need help. Damn biology."

Gordy rounded the table and stopped opposite Sam. They studied each other for a long minute before Gordy took the last steps and sat beside him. Sam's nose wrinkled. Gordy had the faint scent of sweat, bringing back those awful, secret memories. He had to fight the urge to put his hand over his nose to lessen the odor.

"You're in Bio 101, right?" Gordy asked.

Sam pulled his sleeve down his arm and pressed his nose against it. Gordy's funk was all he could think about.

"Yeah, Bio 101 with Hawthorne."

"The labs or the lectures?"

"Both. Some of it I don't get." Sam considered for a minute. "Actually, I don't get most of it. It isn't logical."

Gordy stopped flipping through the textbook and studied Sam. "It is logical. It all follows patterns and systems. What's your major?"

"Computer science. You can't get more structured than that. It's all ones and zeros. I understand it well enough that campus IT hired me."

"Biology is all made of elements. From there, you get molecules and everything else. That's basic."

Sam ground his teeth, losing his nonexistent patience with his overrated tutor. Gordy's odor had expanded and had become a distinctive metallic note on the back of his tongue.

"Okay. According to Dr. Hawthorne's syllabus, you're at the part of the textbook covering cell division. Does that seem about right?"

He slid the opened textbook over to Sam and leaned closer to check the information at the beginning of the chapter. The odor strengthened and the heat coming from Gordy's body was obvious. Sam scrubbed his knuckles across his nose, becoming more frustrated with each passing moment.

Gordy bounced his leg as he explained a particular part of the complicated heredity equation, which Sam understood none of.

"Are you getting this? It's confusing. A lot of people have trouble understanding how it works."

Sam's anger flared again, but he calmed himself. "Yeah, it's not bad. The cells split, the chromosomes split, everything splits. But it's so boring. How do you keep it all in your head?"

Gordy considered him for a moment. "You get the numbers, then. Do the structures make sense to you? Are you having trouble remembering the details?"

Sam knew his face must be bright red. This jock wasn't going to talk to him as if he was a fifth grader. He decided the time had come for him to let Gordy understand how he felt. "Look. I'm good at my major and can remember several computer languages. I wouldn't be taking this stupid biology class if I didn't have to so I can graduate. And what I don't need is attitude from a damn jock."

Gordy pushed away from the table and his shirt billowed then fell against his chest, filling the surrounding air with the musky scent Sam found so offensive. That was the last straw. He lost what tiny amount of decorum he had.

"Oh my God, you stink. You smell like a goat or something. Don't you ever shower?"

Gordy stared at Sam until the tension between them was palpable. His heavy eyebrows twisted together until the space between them almost disappeared. A muscle in his jaw knotted and unknotted so fast that it seemed to jump. His lips pressed together hard until all that remained was a tight slash across his lower face. Gordy dragged the textbook back and it was obvious that only strength of will allowed him to close the book with just a soft thud. He tucked the tome under his arm and started down the aisle.

"That's it? The whiz kid of biology is running off without doing his job? Isn't that just typical? Well, run, Mister Football Stud, and take the funky locker room stink with you."

Gordy stopped, his muscles tensing as he drew in a breath and held it for a minute before turning to Sam. He stalked closer, leaning into Sam until their faces were inches apart. Light flashed across his deep brown eyes, and the amber filigree that surrounded the iris seemed to be molten lava. Sam recognized a trace of mint on Gordy's breath as they glared at each other.

Gordy bit off his first words. "So, you think I stink? Some of us don't have everything handed to us. We have to work to pay for school. You're the one who whined to Connie in the Help Center and said you had to get help *today*. I rearranged my schedule, did my workout early to shower and get here on time. And what you smell is soap. I don't know what your problem is, but it started long before I got here."

Rage, indignation and a slight amount of fear coursed through Sam as he stared at the big linebacker. He refused to let himself be intimidated by their differences in size. He'd never let someone bully him again. "I thought you could be professional and do your job. But I guess if it's not football, you don't give a fuck about it. I'm sure you're already getting paid for this session, so why don't you shuffle off to meet with your no-neck Neanderthal buddies to talk about trying to intimidate the person who paid you to help them."

Gordy's jaw clamped down hard and the bouncing jaw muscle became a fixed point. "Before I lose what little cool I still have left, I'm leaving, but you're an ass."

"At least I'm not a mindless thug who picks on people smaller than them and enjoys it."

Gordy grabbed his bulging backpack and tossed it over

his shoulder as if it were weightless. He turned to Sam again. His expression contained more pity. "You have issues. You should get help."

Rage flared in Sam as Gordy turned and made his way off the floor.

"Wait a minute!" Sam yelled.

"Hey. Keep it down. I'm trying to study for a chem test and I can't concentrate."

Sam glanced in time to see the person who had scolded him disappear behind his desk. By the time he turned back, Gordy was gone.

Sam ground his teeth as he gathered his bag. He would pass this class, and he didn't need the help from a muscle-bound jock.

* * * *

Gordy tried to focus on helping Sarah with the tamales she was making. He'd worked for weeks talking her into making a batch of the labor-intensive treats. He'd eaten them before at various Mexican restaurants but had never been impressed. Then his best friend Nate'd had him over to try the version his then-girlfriend made. They had been delicious. Since then, he'd nagged Sarah constantly for more of the cornhusk-wrapped delicacies.

Sarah peered over his shoulder. "I don't want it too hot. Just melt the lard and it makes it easier to stir with the masa. It's one of the tricks of my tamales."

Gordy stirred the contents of the saucepan carefully before he shot Sarah a grin. "Are you kidding? I've been trying to get you to make more tamales since yours and Nate's wedding. I'm planning to do exactly what you tell me to do"—Gordy's expression tightened—"unlike the idiot who signed up for tutoring today. He was an ass."

"Gordon Hager, watch your mouth," Sarah scolded him.

Gordy rolled his eyes at Nate but apologized. "Sorry, Sarah, but he was. He said I stunk and that I was an ignorant jock. I'll have him know that I'd just showered before going to the library. And it wasn't like I asked him to meet on Sunday. Pis..." He glanced at Sarah as she shredded the pork. "Pulling something like that ticks me off."

"What was his major?"

"Computer science. He said biology didn't make sense."

Nate chuckled as he ate one of the cookies Sarah had made. "The whole school thing isn't as easy for some of us as it is for you."

Gordy rolled his eyes but kept his mouth shut. He concentrated on filling the tamales, folding them and stacking them in the steamer. When the first layer was finished, she turned to Gordy with a smile.

"He was cute, wasn't he? You thought he was cute."

Gordy frowned at her. "That had nothing to do with it. He was such a jerk. It was unbelievable."

Sarah carefully spread a layer of the tamale dough over the cornhusk and handed it to Gordy. After a few minutes passed, Sarah began to talk. "What's he look like?"

Gordy refused to meet her gaze. "I don't know. About my height. Skinny. You know, typical college guy."

Nate came around the counter to help fit the last of the tamales into the steamer. They finished the final layer, put on the lid then Nate carried it to the stove. He turned and wrapped his arms around Sarah and grinned at Gordy. As always, Gordy couldn't keep from thinking what a beautiful couple they made. Nate's muscular body and mahogany coloring were the perfect foil for Sarah's bright red curls and porcelain skin. He started to mention to them again about what a good-looking couple they made, but Nate waved dismissively.

"Stop stalling. What aren't you telling us? You're avoiding the questions more than I did when I was telling my mother I'd proposed to Sarah."

"And how did that go?"

Nate grinned. "We're married. She speaks to us. If we ever have kids, she'll be happier, but then she's that way with my brothers and sisters. And we did go through the whole marriage thing."

"Good information, even if I think my parents will implode when they find out their oldest son likes dudes."

"They did fine when they met your black roommate. Give them a little slack. But you're stalling. What is it about difficult-tutor-boy that makes you grin every time you talk about him?"

Sarah cocked an eyebrow and joined Nate in their showdown. But it didn't take long for Gordy to give in after Sarah glanced over to the tamales with a significant expression.

"All right, fine. You don't have to threaten with the tamales. He's cute, okay? As tall as I am but with a runner's build. There's also an adorable sprinkling of freckles across the bridge of his nose. He's my type in just about every way."

Nate started to ask more questions, but Gordy interrupted him. "Okay, fine. Jeez! He has the sexiest dark-auburn hair. But it doesn't matter how good-looking he is, he was a jerk and I'm not dealing with him again."

By now, Gordy was getting frustrated with his friends, and he thought they were aware of it, too, since the conversation slipped away from his personal life to the safer topics of food and football.

By the time Gordy gathered up his gear to head home, he was stuffed with tamales and had enough in freezer bags to last him for several meals. He pulled his boots on just as Sarah stepped closer and he gave her his usual hug. "Thanks for inviting me over. As always, everything was delicious."

She whispered in his ear before letting him go, "Don't worry about the cute guy. The right man will come along."

Gordy kept his thoughts to himself and gave her a final tight hug.

"Gorrrdeeee!"

Gordy's grin was genuine as he and Nate jumped at each

other. Their chest bump rattled the dishes drying in the sink and sent each of them backward for several feet.

"Boys!" Sarah muttered.

Chapter Two

The soft chatter didn't reach Sam as the other students in his lab section gathered their books and shoved them into bags. His eyes locked on the paper he was holding. The guy sitting next to him — he thought he recalled a name like Mark or something similar — pushed back his metal stool and the rattle that ensued knocked Sam from his stupor.

Mark grabbed his bag and threw it over his shoulder before glancing at Sam's paper. "Ouch! That's harsh. Sorry."

Sam looked up, pulling his thoughts together for a few moments. "Yeah. Blew this one."

"I'd bail, get out of the class. Try to get Hawthorne. I hear he's easier."

"Hawthorne's my prof, and I've got to pass or I can't graduate."

"Stop by the Help Center. They have tutors for everything. I had one before. She was great."

Sam twisted his face into a frown. "Yeah, so I've heard."

Mark glanced at his watch. "Crap! I gotta go. My next class is all the way across campus." He flipped Sam a wave and trotted away.

Sam stuffed his notebooks into his bag and zipped it shut. He threaded his arms through the straps and headed out. The only person left in the room was the teaching assistant who was absorbed in paperwork. Sam waited for a break in the hallway traffic, stepped into the flow of people and made his way down the corridor. Still in shock over failing the quiz, he knew with this grade, his average was so low that he wasn't sure he could pass the class. There were no choices left. He needed help.

Directionless, he was more than halfway across campus and realized he had almost covered the distance to the Help Center. Slowing to a stop, Sam stared at the monolithic red brick building that housed it. A steady stream of people moved through the triple doors. The piece of paper crumpled in his fist was his motivation. The paper was so covered with red it appeared as though whoever had graded the assignment had hit a major artery. He knew what was on the page. The image was burned into his brain.

"Sam? You okay?"

Shaken from his introspection, he glanced over to see the concerned face of a friend. Rachel and he had been tight since they'd met during freshman orientation. A few weeks later, when they had found each other at the first meeting of the campus Gay-Straight Alliance, the friendship had been sealed. She was also the only soul who knew his history.

"Hey, Rachel. Yeah, I'm okay. Having problems with a class. I'm trying to decide if there's a way to still pass."

She glanced at the building a few yards away. "The Help Desk can find you a tutor. That's what I'd do."

"I tried that." He frowned. "They sent a guy who's on the football team."

Rachel took a deep breath that she leaked past her lips. "Sorry, Sam. I know that's a big trigger for you."

"It's nothing to do with triggers. He was a bad tutor."

"Who was it?"

"I don't know. Gordy something. He's on the football team."

"Gordy Hager? Big guy with dark hair and a nice tan?"

"Yeah, something like that. Why?"

"Sam, you need to get out occasionally. That's the guy the university uses as a poster child for the perfect student athlete. Everyone says he's brilliant. He was your tutor?"

Sam rubbed his hands across his face and tried to calm himself so Rachel wouldn't know he was questioning his reactions, even if he was unsure of his control over parts of his response. At least, that's what he told himself.

"If you say so, I guess that's who it was. Sounds like the same guy. Just seemed like a big, dumb jock."

She drew her mouth into a thin line and shrugged. "I hope you find whatever you need."

Sam was trying to think of a reply when another girl ran up to them, grabbed Rachel's hand and pulled her into a kiss. "Come on, Rach. The women's rugby is about to start. You promised you'd go with me."

She grinned and glanced back at Sam. "I'm going to a rugby game. God help us all."

Sam couldn't help but smile and shake his head. He watched as Rachel disappeared around a building and realized he was no closer to finding a solution to his own crisis. *Come on, Sam. You're avoiding this like you're a freshman.* He shook himself and headed to the door of the Help Center.

He made his way through the maze of hallways to discover he still had difficulty finding the office. After a few minutes of searching, he relented and asked directions. Now he homed in on the suite of rooms that held what he needed.

He opened the glass door, walked to the first available staff person and sat down. She typed for a few moments on the keyboard as she studied the paperwork in front of her. She finished with a final click before she turned to Sam with a smile.

"Hi. What can I help you with?"

"Yes, ma'am. I need to sign up for a tutor in Biology 101."

"Okay...let's see who's available." Her fingers flew across the keyboard in a flurry of starts and stops. She stared at the screen for a moment before refocusing on him. "Looks like we only have one. He became available in the last few days." She gave him a genuine smile. "You're in luck. Gordy is our best tutor. He's wonderful at explaining difficult ideas."

"Gordy...Hager?"

"Yes, Gordy Hager."

"Umm, is there anyone else available?"

She studied him for a moment. "No. Gordy is the only biology tutor we have free."

Sam squirmed in the chair, trying to work out the details while the woman's fingers raced again. The pause and her expression were ominous. She cocked her head and pressed her lips together.

"Are you Samuel Doherty?"

Sam's stomach dropped like he was in the lead car on a rollercoaster and left him queasy. "Yes, ma'am. I'm Sam."

"I'm afraid Gordy requested you not be assigned to him. He doesn't believe he can help you."

When he met the woman's gaze, it hadn't changed much. A slight tightening around the lips, a little tilt to her brow, but Sam had no doubt of her opinion of him. *I've got to get help. My biases aside, he seems to know his shit.* His mind raced as he tried to find another solution.

"Is there no one else? I could pay them."

She folded her hands on the counter between them and her expression made it obvious she was finished with him. "No, Samuel. We don't have any biology tutors available. You might talk to the instructor or see if there are study groups you could join."

Stunned, Sam grabbed his bag from the floor where he'd dropped it at some point and made his way out of the door, still reeling. *I'll get help. Wait a minute. Gordy's email address will be in the campus directory. I'll get it and email him to ask for a second chance. If I grovel enough, I'm sure he'll agree to help me.*

* * * *

Sam tapped a pencil against the desk in his room. The next exam was Monday, and it was Thursday. He'd emailed Gordy several days ago, but hadn't gotten a reply. He'd held out for a day before sending the second, then third, message. Each subsequent email had become more pitiful as his desperation grew. He didn't quit trying, but Sam decided his messages were an act of futility. He might as well print them off, smear them with brown mustard and eat them, for all the good they were doing.

I may go down in flames, but I won't quit trying.

He worked through the last chapter the professor had assigned, making notes as he went, trying to understand the highlights. But no matter how hard he tried, it all mushed together. Each piece didn't make sense with all the others. The most frustrating part was that he sensed the key points were close but he couldn't make those final, critical connections.

He shoved away from his desk, fighting to keep from throwing the book out the window. He paced the room, his arms and legs shaking as he tried to relax.

His email chimed.

Sam dove for the computer, frantic to see if this was the email he needed. He saw the title.

Message from 'Hager, Gordon'.

Sam's stomach knotted and the taste of bile filled his mouth. After freezing for a second, he clicked the message.

Dear Sam,

I've been out of town working on my senior honors project in a remote part of southeastern Oklahoma. We were gathering data for several days and I returned a few hours ago.

I was surprised to find your emails. I thought you were clear about your feelings regarding me serving as your tutor. I checked with local experts who confirmed that hell, in fact, has not frozen over. The threat of failing has made people do things more desperate than working with someone they despise.

Regardless, I'm afraid my research has been sped up and I no longer can take on another tutoring assignment.

Best of luck with your course.

Sincerely,

Gordon Hager

Sam's chest constricted and his nausea grew with each word. His heart sank into the ground by the time he'd read it over again. He took a deep breath and fought down his rocketing fear.

"Hey, Sam. You okay in there?" yelled one of his suite mates.

He swallowed hard before he replied. "I'm good. No problem."

A plan burst into his head. Well, a half-baked possible fiasco that might be illegal and was certainly immoral. But, at this point, he didn't care. He needed help, and everyone seemed to think Gordy was the best.

Sam walked through the crap covering his floor and made his way to the doorway. He looked around and spotted the person he was trying to find.

"Hey, Rob. Do you still have a cousin who works in the Help Center office?"

Rob studied him. "Yeah. Why? What are you up to this time?"

"Didn't I introduce you to a friend of mine? And aren't you dating her now?"

"Yes, Sam. You introduced me to Laura, and we have been going out for several weeks."

Sam gave him an innocent smile.

Chapter Three

Sam wrapped his knuckles around the steering wheel of his Volkswagen bug. He'd got Gordy's phone number and address from Rob's cousin. Sam considered trying to call and talk to Gordy, but he decided he'd have more of a chance of getting him to help if he showed up unannounced and begged for pity.

He'd also been lucky. One girl who worked at the center remembered what kind of pickup Gordy drove. He'd hoped that was enough information. But then he raced down the third large hill heading into the less populated parts of the surrounding county and lost his cell phone connection. Sam thought he was close, and he'd spot the red four-by-four dually Gordy drove parked at one of the houses with no problem.

He'd been wrong.

Sam covered more miles, several over roads with only a gravel surface, but nothing met his description of Gordy's vehicle. There were too many houses with pickups in the front yard and a huge dog chained beside the back door. He'd long ago left the roads maintained by the city and soon he'd be down to paths too rough for his little car. It was getting dark, and he was running out of choices. He swallowed any pride he had left.

He pulled to the side of the road, dug in his pocket and brought out the folded piece of paper with Gordy's contact information. He sighed as he opened it, keyed the number in and waited. On the third ring, someone answered the phone.

"Hello."

"Hi. Could I speak with Gordy?"

"This is Gordy. Who's this?"

"Hey. I don't know if you remember me. I'm Sam Doherty and—"

The line went dead. Sam stared at the phone, amused more than anything. He redialed and waited. It rang several times then rolled to voice mail. Sam considered leaving a message but discarded the idea and hung up. Determination filled him and he dialed again.

About fifteen minutes, and twenty calls later, Gordy answered the phone again, "You know I could block you?"

"Hang on! Let me talk for a minute. If you say no, I'll quit bothering you," Sam said.

"You've got one minute."

Sam talked as fast as he could get the words out. "First, I'm sorry for being such a jerk. It was a bad day, I guess. But you didn't deserve me unloading on you. So, sorry. But I'm desperate. I have to pass the intro bio this semester and the other one next semester. The people at the Help Center said you were the best tutor. I'll find a way to pay you if that's what it takes, or I can take care of keeping your computer working right. But I need help."

He took a deep breath. "Please."

No sound came out and Sam worried. When he couldn't take the pressure any longer he spoke into the phone. "Gordy?"

"There are a bunch of things I need to do around here first. I wasn't kidding, and I need to work on my research project."

Sam jumped at the opening. "I can help you do whatever you need. But I need a tutor for this class."

There was a tone in Gordy's voice that made Sam wonder if he might regret the deal he was hatching. "Well, I wouldn't mind having some help with my computer that's messing up. But more important, it's my weekend to take samples from the research steers. If you help me with the computer and the cattle, I'll help you."

"It's a deal. How do I get to your house?"

About twenty minutes later, he was parking his dust-covered Beetle in front of a low-slung ranch. He glanced around but saw nothing unusual. The red-brick house was more contemporary than most with fences and corrals along with a red barn situated beyond the first set of gates. It didn't seem like where a college student would be living. He walked to the front door and reached toward the doorbell.

"Looks like you found the place."

Startled, he lowered his hand and turned to find Gordy standing at the corner of the house. His heart hammered, but he'd be damned if he would let Gordy find out he had rattled him.

"Yeah, it was simple with your directions. But it is off the beaten path." He motioned to the house. "Upscale place for a college student."

Gordy shot a fast glance at him, the corner of his mouth quirking upward. "I don't live in the house. One of my profs and his family live there. I'm camping out in the travel trailer in back. I trade living in it for helping with their place."

He studied Sam for a minute until Sam was feeling underdressed in jeans, T-shirt and runners.

"We'll get you a pair of rubber boots at the shed. Otherwise, you'll ruin your tenny runners."

Sam twisted his lips and questioned his sanity in agreeing to help with Gordy's research. Not many of the projects Sam was familiar with needed rubber boots. He wasn't a big fan of the whole outdoors thing, either. But he'd already agreed, and he wasn't getting a second chance with Gordy. *Really it would be more like a third chance. No, I don't see that happening.*

Sam nodded and made certain to wipe any expression of distaste from his face. He must have failed miserably since Gordy burst out laughing. He frowned at the football player. Before he could say anything, Gordy began.

"Okay, this will be interesting. Because as bad as you think this is going to be, it'll be worse." Without giving Sam time to protest, Gordy tossed an equipment box into the pickup bed and jumped into the front seat. He rolled down the power windows and yelled out to Sam.

"You coming? Or do you not need a tutor now?"

Sam clenched his jaws and snorted an angry breath through his nose. But he trotted to the passenger door and crawled into the huge vehicle. A moment later they were roaring down the highway to one of the research centers the ag college kept. He wasn't sure what to say, so he kept quiet, and Gordy seemed to be focused on the trip.

They pulled into the center and wound their way through the maze of gravel roads until they came to a stop at a large, green-metal shed. Sam stood peering over row after row of white pipe and cable fences dotted with metal buildings of every size. It reminded Sam a little of an anthill with all the activity going on.

"Ready?" Gordy asked.

Sam walked over, checked out what Gordy had in his arms and shot him a questioning glance. Gordy gave him a grin in response. "Rubber boots and AI gloves."

Sam hopped around and changed out his trainers for the boots that went to his knees. By the time he'd donned different shoes, Gordy had a small group of cattle in the pen. With a rattle and a bang the heavy metal gate closed, and Gordy walked over to Sam. He pointed to the bucket of feed. "Take that and pour a little of what's in it into each feed pan. I'll close the rails behind them as they go into their stalls."

Sam looked at the huge animals, then at the narrow pens Gordy seemed to think they would go into. "Just put a little in each one?"

"Yup, they know what's going on. They'll go in without trouble."

Sam shrugged and started down the row of constrictive stalls. There was a clang as a bar slid in place behind each animal. By the time he reached the last stall, Gordy was sliding its closure shut. He disappeared into the room at the end of the shed, came out with a stack of cups and a smile Sam didn't like at all. He stood watching as Gordy put on one glove that came to his shoulder. *Why do I think I should have asked what AI meant?*

"Okay, so today I'm taking fecal samples, and I'll show you how to—"

"We're doing *what?*"

"Samples. To check how they are digesting the wheat pasture."

"Poop? We're picking up *shit?*" The manure smell overwhelmed him, and he gagged.

Gordy chuckled. "Not picking it up so much as catching it."

"Oh God."

The smile on Gordy's face was demonic as he motioned Sam over. Sam gritted his teeth, determined to do what he'd agreed to do. He listened as Gordy explained how to capture the manure fresh from its source, transfer it to one of the sample containers then write the ear tag number across the top. He set the finished product in a box he'd brought from the pickup before turning to Sam.

"Easy, huh? You do the next one, and I'll make sure you don't hurt the steer."

Sam pulled the glove to his shoulder and stepped within reach of the next animal. Gordy moved its tail to one side and Sam swallowed hard, trying to keep from losing his lunch. But he would not lose his tutor because he couldn't stand touching the animal's butt.

He reached forward, fighting to keep from puking, his arm shaking.

Gordy gripped Sam's wrist. "That's enough. I think it's gross, too. You must need help bad if you'd help collect samples."

A sense of relief washed over Sam, but he also would fulfil his part of the bargain. "Hey, I can still help. I mean, this is a real thing you need to do, right?"

Gordy cocked an eyebrow and studied him for a minute. From the expression on his face, Sam hoped Gordy was impressed by what he'd said. Sam believed Gordy was a man who valued honesty and the willingness to work.

With a nod, he explained, "Yeah, it's a real thing. How about if you mark the sample? That would help keep everything clean."

Sam nodded, determined to carry out his end of the bargain. Gordy handed him the first sealed sample. He felt the hot container, and hurled.

* * * *

They rolled to a stop in front of Gordy's trailer and sat quietly for a minute. Sam was still a little queasy, but he was proud that after puking, he'd helped finish. The first thing he would do when he got to his room was shower until he'd scrubbed off the funky smell. But for now, he'd earned his tutoring session, even if he had been a jerk the first time.

"Sorry about that. I've never had someone throw up before," Gordy said.

"I probably should have told you that I had a weak stomach."

Gordy chuckled as he climbed out of the truck. "Let's get going. We can get some studying finished before I have to check on the animals."

Sam trotted to his car, pulled out his book bag then raced to catch up with Gordy, who'd paused at the door and glanced back. But he opened the trailer and motioned Sam inside. "The table is on the right. Spread out there. Just push my stuff to the side."

Sam moved through the tiny space and found where Gordy had sent him. He gazed around in awe at the immaculate home—no piles of clothes or dirty dishes. It looked like a staged living area at one of those garden shows they held at the fairgrounds each year. The counters were spotless, and the bathroom was just as orderly. As he checked out the room, he realized Gordy was staring at him.

"It's not much. But like I said, it's cheap."

"No, not at all. I was thinking what a mess my room was in comparison."

Gordy shrugged and his face flushed, but ignored the direction the conversation had taken. "You said you have Hawthorne?"

"Yeah, we had a lab test, and I didn't do so well."

"How bad is 'not so well'?"

"Fucked up beyond belief?"

Gordy chuckled but didn't comment any further. He flipped through Sam's textbook until he reached the pages he'd been searching for. "Okay, so you should be covering the heredity section?"

Sam gave him a nod.

"Good. Let's start with simple genetics, just a single gene. Like eye color in people" — he grinned at Sam — "which isn't that simple. But for the sake of the assignment…"

Gordy started through the basic concepts. Sam realized Gordy needed to find out how much he knew. He was surprised he remembered as much as he did.

The next few hours were spent coaxing Sam through the more complex lessons. Sam hated to admit it, but Gordy was an outstanding tutor. They worked through another section until Sam had it down. Almost giddy, he jumped to his feet and did a victory dance. When Gordy laughed, Sam turned and gave him a double high-five.

"Damn! You *are* the master tutor." He remembered that Gordy had his own long to-do list and glanced outside to see the sun disappearing. He turned back to Gordy. "It's late. Let me help you. I can check your computer later."

"It's okay. It won't take me too long."

"No, honest. What can I do to help?" Sam paused for a minute. "Nothing needs sampled, does it?"

Gordy laughed and shook his head. "No, nothing else

needs sampled. Besides, the animals here are more Steve's pets. But I guess you would help me finish quicker. I have a couple of baby goats that need a bottle."

"The goats are how big?" Sam asked.

"You know, babies. Really little." Gordy held out his hands separated by about ten inches.

"Oh yeah. I can do that."

"Cool! Their bottles are in the fridge. Just run hot water over them for a few minutes to warm up the formula. They're in a horse stall. It's just the two of them."

Sam nodded. This sounded more up his alley. He waited for Gordy to leave then started to warm up the bottles. It took longer than he expected, but several minutes later, they had warmed and Sam headed off in search of his assignment. He knew where the goats were when he flipped on the lights, and they began complaining. It must have been past their mealtime. They were voicing their displeasure at the lack of service. Sam headed toward the din, opened the door and two tiny four-legged creatures with the ferocity of a piranha attacked him.

"Hey, hey. Calm down. I'm here."

Sam swung a bottle to each one. They both immediately began nursing like fiends, making sucking noises that filled the building. Sam slipped to his knees to make feeding the two eating machines easier. Their tails were wagging like signal flags and their long ears swung with their vigorous nursing.

It didn't take long for them to drain their bottles. As soon as they did, they climbed over him, trying to see if he had anything else edible. One had his front hooves on Sam's shoulder nibbling at his ear while the other was nursing a fold in his T-shirt. He chuckled when the low-ranging truant found something very interesting on Sam — a nipple.

"Hey! No biting the nipples. Only hot boyfriends get those."

"He seems to like doing that. I wear a jacket when I feed them."

Heat flashed across Sam's skin and a knot formed in his stomach. But Gordy said nothing about his comment. He squatted down and gave the two a few minutes' attention before carrying them back into the stall and turning to Sam.

"Hey, thanks. That saved me a lot of time. Those two are high maintenance."

Sam still felt the heat of his embarrassment as he followed Gordy out the door. They went into the trailer. Sam gathered his stuff and shoved it into his bag. He didn't want to leave. He wasn't sure why, because he had no interest in a relationship with anyone. But he wanted to spend more time with Gordy. He had to try.

"Hey, it's late and I'm starving. You interested in grabbing a bite? We could go to Joe's. My treat."

Gordy gave him a look he couldn't interpret that shifted to a slight frown. "Sorry, but I'll have to take a rain check. I have too much to do tonight."

The walls that Sam had lowered shot back up. "Yeah. Sure. Some other time." He tossed the bag over one shoulder and started out the door. "Oh crap, I didn't fix your computer."

"Don't sweat it. You can check it next time."

Sam nodded, turning before he reached the door. "I'll probably need more help. Can I call you?"

Sam swore Gordy's expression brightened. "Sure. Anytime."

He nodded then made his way to the bug as fast as possible. His emotions were such a convoluted mess that he made no attempt to sort them from each other.

Chapter Four

Gordy stood in the shadowed doorway to the barn watching Sam park his bright blue beetle next to his pickup. He was still trying to figure Sam out. At their first meeting in the library, he'd been a complete ass. But a few days later he'd returned, begging for help. He knew Sam had gone back to the Help Center and asked for someone else. Connie had filled Gordy in on the details and dismissed Sam as another spoiled rich kid. The flood of emails had been annoying, but Gordy had to admire his determination. The barrage of calls asking for directions, though? If he needed help that bad, Gordy would give him a second chance.

That he'd been willing to help Gordy with sample collection… Well, no one had ever helped him with that chore before. He'd grown on Gordy. When he saw Sam making his way to the trailer, Gordy couldn't resist a little teasing. He ran back, opened the gate to the goats' stall and raced back to the door with the pair. They glanced at Gordy for a moment before doing what he'd hoped. They bounced across the yard and headed straight for Sam.

"Hey, guys!"

I'll explain the gender of the two at some point.

Sam sat on the ground and let them climb over him while he scratched behind their floppy ears. Gordy found the sight endearing and let them continue for a few minutes before stepping closer. As happened more frequently with Sam, Gordy felt a flutter in his stomach as he watched.

"They seem to like you."

Sam looked up and grinned. "They came running out to meet me." He cocked an eye toward Gordy. "You let them out."

Gordy plastered an innocent expression on his face. "Me? I'd never do something like that."

Sam hesitated as if he took Gordy's comment as fact. "Yeah, okay." Gordy winked at him, and Sam burst into a grin. He stood, scooped up the animals and headed toward the barn with Gordy at his side. Once they had the two troublemakers secure in their stall, he turned to Gordy.

"You sure you don't mind helping me again? I've got a quiz tomorrow, and I'd really appreciate whatever you have time to do."

Gordy gave a shrug as they made their way to his home, "Sure. I've got biochem homework, too. We're going through neurotoxins. Mostly it's memorizing things. But I might get you to quiz me. I use notecards when I study, so it shouldn't be that bad."

Sam's smile got even larger. "Sure! I'd be happy to help."

"Cool. Give me a few minutes to shower. I've got pop in the fridge." Gordy swung open the door and motioned Sam inside. Sam grabbed a can from the refrigerator, sat at the table and spread out his classwork.

Unconcerned, Gordy pulled his sweaty T-shirt over his head and wiped off his torso with it. When he glanced up, Sam's gaze was locked on him. A flash of embarrassment washed over Gordy. "Sorry. I didn't even think about stripping in front of you. No one else is ever here, and I guess I've gotten comfortable undressing and knowing no one will care. Sorry."

Sam gave a dismissive wave. "Don't sweat it. It's not a big deal. It's your place. Do whatever you feel comfortable."

"Cool. I'm used to locker rooms, so I'll try to at least use a towel to cover the goods."

Sam found something fascinating in his textbook. "Sure. Whatever. It's cool. I'll reread the last chapter."

Gordy nodded and worked at stripping off the rest of his clothes. As he stepped out of his underwear, he scratched his balls before wrapping a huge, thick towel around his waist. He glanced up and found Sam still absorbed in his textbook. He tossed his dirty clothes into the hamper. "It won't take me long. I've learned to shower fast."

"That's fine. Take your time," Sam said.

Gordy slid the door shut behind him, hung his towel on the side and lathered up. He couldn't help but remember Sam's first tirade about how he smelled, and he attempted to wash every square inch of his body. The water was cooling when he finished. He turned off the shower and tried to dry himself in the microscopic bathroom but kept banging his elbows against the walls.

This is ridiculous. If he's going to hang around, I don't want to be self-conscious.

Gordy stepped out and ran the towel over himself. He lifted one leg to dry his junk then wrapped the towel back around his waist before looking at Sam.

Sam stared at Gordy and his pale cheeks were as red as the circles they painted on the Christmas nutcrackers. Gordy considered for a minute but decided he was finished apologizing for what he did in his own home.

He made his way to the bedroom, and didn't bother to close the door as he dropped his damp towel into the hamper. He slipped on a pair of briefs, workout shorts and a jersey. Gordy pulled the tail of the shirt down as he walked back toward Sam.

"Okay, I'm clean and we both need to study." Gordy opened his book and started through the biochem on next week's test. Sam's flushed cheeks had disappeared and he seemed focused on the bio chapter.

Several hours later, he realized Sam had only asked a few questions but he'd read the same section multiple times. He waited for a few minutes before he asked. "You confused over something?"

"These single nucleotide polymorphism things. I'm just not getting their purpose."

"Oh yeah. That's where they found the gay gene," Gordy said.

"The gay *what*?"

Gordy felt his stomach knot. *How do I answer his question and not out myself?*

"Ah, yeah. Not really a single gene. More like a location on the X and number eight chromosomes. A band in the genome." Gordy said, stumbling on the last few words as he saw Sam's expression harden. He tried to continue, "You know, to show being gay isn't a choice."

Gordy wanted to escape, hide from this mess he had created. He'd only shared this hidden part of his life with a few people. From the hard, disgusted expression on Sam's face, he was afraid he'd given away his secret to the wrong person. He didn't need difficulties right now.

He was still trying to find something to say when he realized Sam was speaking. "It's not a choice. Just ask anyone who's gay."

There was silence for a few minutes as Gordy's thoughts raced in a dozen different directions. He was about to change the conversation when Sam began. "You might as well know that I'm gay. It's no secret. I'm out to everyone. My family has known for years."

Gordy struggled to connect everything Sam had just said. *What should I do? What do I say? I don't know when I'll come out, but I need to be past college, especially beyond the coach's reach.*

When he changed his focus from himself, he realized Sam had just shared a personal bit of information and Gordy had left him waiting for an answer. Even worse, Sam was furious and on his way out the door.

"Sam. Wait. Hey, hang on. You caught me by surprise. I mean—"

Sam yanked open the door of his car, tossed his bag in then dropped into the seat. Gordy stepped closer, blocking the door from closing. Sam yanked on the handle, bouncing the door off his hip.

"Come on. Give me a minute. I think it's great you're gay. It's just…"

"I get it. I've seen the look before. Get out of my way or I swear to God I'll run over your ass."

"Come on, man. Give me a—"

Sam slipped the bug into drive and floored it. Gordy held on for a few lurching steps before Sam shot past him. The last he saw of Sam was the blue car fishtailing through the gravel on the county road and disappearing a few seconds later.

* * * *

Sam paced his room, kicking each object out of his way as it crossed his path. He swung at a pair of pants and missed. "Damn it! Get out of my fucking way!"

"That's it. Beat the hell out of the innocent khakis. What did they ever do to you?"

He glanced up to see Rachel with her arms crossed standing in the doorway to his room. "Not a great time, Rach. I'm pissed off."

"I assumed that when a pair of your favorite sexy undies came flying out the door." She twirled a pair of aqua-colored low-rise briefs on her index finger and smirked.

Sam grinned. "Just an FYI. I have no idea if those are clean or not."

Rachel threw the underwear at Sam. "Eww! Boys are so disgusting!"

Sam chuckled for a moment then flopped onto his bed. Rachel stared at him for a minute before sitting on its side. "What happened? Weren't you going to work with the football player tutor?"

Sam stuck his hands behind his head and blew air through his nose. "I made the mistake of telling him I was gay."

"Why'd you do that?"

"Hell, I don't know. Somehow, we were talking about heredity and about gay being a choice, and boom, it rolled out of my mouth."

"Wow, and you already had problems with the guy.

Sorry to hear that, Sam. At least you aren't falling for him or anything."

Sam sat quietly for several minutes as he thought about seeing Gordy—naked Gordy. He ran his tongue over his lips at the memory of his tight, round butt.

"Oh my God. You fell for him. You hate jocks—any jocks. After all the drunken tirades you've made me listen to about how worthless jocks are to the planet, you've fallen for one."

"What? No! I haven't fallen for a damn jock. Good grief, Rachel. Where did you get that idea? He's just a waste of good DNA."

His best friend leaned over and playfully wiped the corners of his mouth. "You seem to be drooling over the hot muscle-guy."

Sam gave her a scornful glare, even as he tried to ignore the knot in his stomach every time he replayed the scene of Gordy drying himself. When he recalled Gordy's reaction to Sam coming out to him, the attraction evaporated.

The excitement drained from his system and he rolled to his side. "It doesn't matter what feelings I have. He's not into the whole gay-friend thing, much less anything more. You should have seen his face."

They sat together commiserating in mutual silence for several minutes before Sam decided they'd wasted enough time being maudlin. "So, speaking of people who think jocks are hot. How was the women's rugby game?"

Rachel fanned herself. "Oh good lord. Those were hot girls. I'd let a couple of them toss me around the bed."

Sam laughed and listened to his friend recount the blow by blow of the game from the perspective of someone who didn't understand how to play it. It helped distract him from the lump sitting in his stomach. But then, he wouldn't put it past Rachel to make up parts of the story to help distract him.

Chapter Five

Sam stared at his quiz in shock. Dark red ink decorated the corner of the paper with a B. *I made a B. On a biology quiz. Holy shit...*

The guy next to Sam leaned over and checked out his score. "Hey, congrats, man. That's better than I did. I'm failing. How'd you get a better score?"

Sam sat absorbing the information for a moment before he realized someone was talking with him. "Sorry. What'd you say?"

"This class is kicking my ass. How'd you do so much better?"

Sam nodded, trying to find his voice. "I got a tutor."

"Damn, maybe I should get one. They sure helped your grades."

Sam shrugged. "Yeah, I guess so."

"Yup, I'll have to check into that."

Sam realized a little later that the students for the next class were filing into the surrounding seats. He slipped everything into his backpack and made his way out of the room. He headed to his normal lunchtime haunt, and the growl from his stomach reinforced that it was ready to be filled.

A few minutes later he stood in the middle of the food court at the Student Union, trying to decide what he wanted. Unable to find something new that sounded appetizing, he went for his usual — salad by the ounce. He paid for his meal and searched for a place to sit.

He scanned the area and froze. *Gordy*. He wanted to scream and run away so he didn't need to listen to weak excuses about Gordy's response. He spun and made his way toward an exit.

"Sam. Hey, Sam!"

He slowed to a stop before turning to see what Gordy wanted.

"Hey, Gordy. How are things?"

Gordy scanned the area as if to verify no one could overhear their conversation. He turned to Sam. "Hey, I wanted to talk to you. I called a couple of times but you never called me back."

"Yeah, it's been crazy. Sorry."

"I didn't mean to make you feel bad. I was honored you shared that you were gay with me."

Great. Gordy's researched how to be a good ally. "Don't sweat it. I'm out to everyone, so it's not like it's a big deal."

Gordy refused to meet Sam's gaze. "Yeah, it's complicated…"

"Whatever, Gordy. I understand you have to protect your rep as the perfect student and homophobic jock."

Gordy reached out, almost touching Sam's shoulder. "Hey, no. It isn't like that."

As Sam considered what Gordy had just said, a group of students dressed head to toe in athletic gear walked past. "Hey, Gordy. You ready to go, man? We have to hit the weight room."

Gordy looked distressed as he glanced between the two of them. He thought Gordy might say something, but he dropped his shoulders and left with the group.

Sam couldn't imagine anywhere he wanted to be less.

* * * *

Sam answered questions about the group's activities at their latest Gay-Straight Alliance meeting. As president of the group, he got the majority of the questions, but that was okay with him. He put on his best face and listened to each one carefully. Some people here weren't out. Others were out only to a few people. Not everyone was as fortunate as Sam. Tonight's program had been on safer sex, so there were more questions than usual. Because of the topic, they'd also had several new people attend. The one talking to Sam now was particularly nervous.

"Yeah, so tonight was cool. It's always good to be careful. Right?"

Sam nodded in agreement. "It is. Glad you enjoyed the meeting."

The guy looked nervous and glanced around. "You don't, like, take people's names or anything."

"Well, we keep track of who comes, but we never ask questions about anyone's private life."

"Oh. Yeah. I mean it's all cool. I..."

Sam gave him the most supportive smile he was able to conjure. "I understand. You'll find nothing but support here."

"Sorry. I'm being all weird. But I'm on the baseball team and I can't give them any reason to pull my scholarship."

Sam shook his head. "No, they absolutely can't do that. University policy won't let them discriminate based on sexual orientation."

The guy shook his head, dismissing Sam's statement. "Sports are the last of the good old boys' clubs. They couldn't do it in the open, but they'd say I wasn't playing well and the other players would screw me over."

Rachel appeared at his side. "Hey, Sam. Do we have any more of the safer sex kits with condoms and lube?"

"No, the ones we brought are all gone. The LGBT Office has more. They can stop by and pick up whatever they need." She nodded and moved back to the student she'd been talking with. When he turned back, the kid he'd been visiting with had disappeared. He searched for him, but the room was almost empty. Sam felt like he'd failed the guy.

"Looks like everyone's gone. Nothing like explaining safer sex to have people fornicating like bunnies."

Sam chuckled at Rachel. "Fornicating like bunnies?

There's an interesting image."

"Just because some of us are monks doesn't mean everyone is."

Sam frowned and gave Rachel a scathing glance.

"Okay, sorry. Shouldn't have gone there."

"No, you shouldn't." He glanced around the room. "Looks like it's over. You okay to get home?"

"Yeah, I have a study group upstairs in a few minutes. I'll grab a coffee and head up," Rachel said.

"Hey, who left this?" Sam picked up a rainbow flag about the size of his hand.

"I have no idea. I guess we should keep track of it." She plucked it from his hand and used the safety pins already on each corner to attach it to Sam's backpack. "There you go. You're the rainbow."

Sam checked the room and waved her ahead of him as he pulled the door shut behind them. They parted with a hug and Sam left the Student Union and headed toward his dorm. He'd been walking a few minutes when he realized how deserted campus was. The rows of lights seemed dimmer than usual. He rarely felt uncomfortable being on campus at night, but tonight was becoming an exception. His spidey sense was off the scale for creepy when he heard footsteps behind him.

* * * *

Gordy was leaving the Student Union when he noticed a familiar form in front of him. He'd been trying to talk with Sam after the disaster of a conversation at the Student Union. His friends'd had the worst possible timing, but Sam was also being difficult. Not that Gordy blamed him. If he'd shared something like that, he would have expected a little more support, too.

He rushed to catch up with Sam, hoping to find him with no one around so they could talk. But as he got closer, a handful of figures appeared around Sam. Gordy slowed as he noticed Sam tense. While he couldn't hear what was being said, Sam was getting louder. Gordy's concern grew, and he broke into a run as two of the people lunged toward Sam.

"Grab him!" he heard.

Fury flashed through Gordy as he covered the last few yards and slammed into one of the guys holding Sam, knocking him to the ground. Gordy jumped to his feet and ran at the other one while yelling at the top of his voice. "Call the cops! Someone call the cops!"

Just before they collided, Sam moved, stepped closer and the other guy dropped to his knees. Gordy changed his target and ran at the apparent leader. The guy sprinted away, but Gordy had run down far too many quarterbacks for that to work. Once he was within striking distance, he leaped at the man, grabbed him around the knees and bounced him against the hard ground.

Gordy lifted himself off his catch and saw Sam had the other guy in a hold. A moment later red and blue lights and screaming sirens filled the area. It wasn't much afterward before the police interviewed him and Sam.

It surprised Gordy to find out the police had been searching for the attackers. They'd robbed a few other students on campus, too. Campus police apparently had a campaign to warn students about being alone after dark. Gordy was pleased with himself until he saw Sam stomping toward him.

"What the hell were you doing? I didn't need to be rescued!"

Gordy dropped his jaw as any reply left his head. He stared in disbelief. He was even more shocked when Sam stepped closer and thumped his finger in the middle of Gordy's chest. "I'll let you know if I need your help. Otherwise, assume I'm good. You got it?"

Gordy was so shocked he didn't feel much of anything. He nodded and took a step back. "Sorry, Sam. I switched into 'help my friend' mode. I never was trying to overstep your boundaries."

Sam hesitated for a minute and seemed to have lost some of his bluster. "Yeah, okay. I didn't need help, just for the record."

Sam spun and disappeared into the nearest building, leaving Gordy with a swirl of emotions ranging from anger to guilt.

I can't figure out what he wants.

Chapter Six

Sam sat in his car, looking at the dusting of snow that had softened the early winter landscape, if only for a short time. Light shone through the windows in Gordy's little trailer. It had a charming quality Sam might not have noticed another time. The gray of dusk hid the less appealing details of the surroundings.

He had no need to draw this out further. He hadn't tried to call or email, needing to apologize face-to-face. Sam also hated to admit it, but Gordy identifying him as a friend had more of an impact than he'd thought it would. It shocked him that the straight jock would consider him a friend at all. He had so few. Gordy had come to his aid, and Sam chewed him out about it. Now he'd see if diplomatic skills could save him. The other thing was that Sam still needed Gordy as a tutor. He'd taken a practice exam… He needed help. Sam hoped to repair his friendship and save his grade.

He opened the car door and stepped out. As he approached the tiny home, he smiled at the scene through the window. Gordy was whistling as he did dishes. Sam waited for a minute before knocking, not wanting to ruin such a peaceful scene. But he braced himself and rapped on the door.

The whistling stopped and Gordy froze. Sam waited a moment then knocked again. Gordy grabbed the dishtowel from his shoulder and dried his hands as he moved to the door. It popped open, and Sam stood speechless as his heart hammered in his chest and his mouth went dry. Gordy's expression soured.

"What are you doing here?"

"I owe you an apology for the other day. I was really crappy."

Gordy stood staring, not threatening, but not welcoming. The silence became tense and Gordy shuffled his boots as they stood appraising each other. Then Gordy shook his head and said, "You seem good at putting your foot in your mouth, like up to your thigh."

Sam bit back his first response, which would have been a poor choice. Instead he decided a small dose of honesty would be appropriate. "I have a few issues. Jocks are one of them. Defending myself is another. Neither of them is your fault. Sorry you seem to keep catching the brunt of my hang-ups."

Gordy relaxed, and stepped away from the doorway. "Come in. It's warmer inside."

Sam hesitated, but he needed to be certain. "You sure you want to be alone with a gay guy? You didn't seem to thrilled when I told you I was gay."

Gordy tightened his lips. "Like you said, everybody has issues. Let's just say I have no problem with you being gay and leave it at that. Okay?"

Sam studied him for a minute before nodding. "Okay. I think that's only fair. I'll try to keep everything in check." He hesitated for a moment.

"What? There's more?" Gordy asked.

Sam made vague motions toward his car. "I have my books…"

Gordy chuckled. "Get your stuff. I was cleaning up from dinner, but if you're hungry…" He looked at Sam.

"No. I'm good. I'll grab my backpack." He trotted to his car and returned in a few minutes to spread his material over the table. Gordy was busy putting away the final few things in the kitchen and Sam couldn't help but remember the strip show Gordy had given him the last time he'd been there. Sam realized his fantasizing had left him with a hard cock that could serve as a tent pole. He swallowed hard and refocused on his classwork. Nothing could kill his erection faster than biology.

There was a bang as the cabinet closed, and Gordy sat opposite him. A minute later, textbooks and notes covered the entire surface and both of them focused on their studies.

After a little while, Sam noticed Gordy was becoming frustrated with his computer. When his finger on the Enter key sounded more like a hammer against an anvil, Sam stopped his reading and grinned at Gordy.

"Do you want me to take a look at it before you stick your finger through the keyboard?"

Gordy hesitated for a second but handed the computer over to Sam. "It keeps locking up. If I lose the paper I'm working on, I'm going to be so pissed."

Without another word, Sam turned the computer and started speed typing. In a few seconds, he had the console screen open and was rapid-firing commands on Gordy's computer. He had a suspicion what was happening, and his first test scripts confirmed his suspicions. A few more bursts of commands and he turned the machine back to Gordy.

"Give it a try. I think it's fixed now."

Gordy made a few hesitant keystrokes then shot Sam a triumphant look. "It's working! That's amazing. I've spent hours on the phone with tech support and they hadn't been able to fix it."

Sam gave Gordy a wink. "I told you I was good."

Gordy shook his head then focused on his work.

They'd been studying for quite some time when Gordy leaned back and stretched. As his shirt slid upward, Sam couldn't help but see the fan of dark hair across his slightly rounded stomach. He detected a hint of the smell that set him off when they first met, but now it didn't bother him. In fact, he found it appealing.

Sam scolded himself. He didn't intend to offend his very straight, very large tutor. The stretch went on and Sam allowed himself a few more glimpses of Gordy's massive body. With a groan, Gordy dropped his arms and sighed.

"I'm ready for a break. I need to check on the animals, anyway," Gordy said.

Sam grinned at the memories. After last time, he'd discovered he liked the animals. Well, he liked the goats. The others he wasn't as sure about. But one thing he was certain of, helping with the animals would score him points with Gordy. "Hey, that sounds like a great idea. I can take care of the goats again if that would help." It seemed to Sam as if he were picking what was easy. "Or whatever. But a break sounds good." He shot Gordy his best smile.

"If you'd take care of those four-legged eating machines, that'd be a big help. I'll feed and water everything else."

Sam relaxed and let his happiness show through his carefully constructed expression. "That's cool. I like the little floppy-eared characters."

Gordy handed him two bottles from the fridge before pulling on his boots. Sam glanced over to Gordy while he warmed the bottles and licked his lips as Gordy's muscular butt flexed. Gordy stood first on one leg then on the other. His butt cheeks bulged and stretched his jeans to their limits. When Gordy shot him a smile, Sam returned it without comment.

Gordy said, "If you get done first, I'll be in the barn. One horse has a limp, and it takes more time to check on her."

Sam nodded and followed him out the door. Gordy headed to the red barn at the center of all the pens while Sam trotted to the smaller building that served as the stable and held his favorite goats.

The kids were dancing around his feet by the time he stepped into the stall. He grinned at the aggressive little creatures as they suckled the bottles with a vengeance. Soon there was no more milk, and the gluttons were begging for more.

"Oh hush. You drained those bottles like little pigs. You have plenty to eat around here." Sam gave the pair fresh water and another piece of hay. He closed and latched the stall door and made his way to the barn. He stood just inside the door, letting his eyes adjust to the dim light.

"Hey, Sam. I'm over here checking Molly's hoof," Gordy said.

Sam followed the voice to find Gordy standing beside a huge horse with its foot on his thigh. He dug at the hoof for several minutes, studying it at intervals until he was satisfied. He glanced toward Sam.

"Would you grab a piece of alfalfa and put it in her feeder?"

"Sure." Sam pulled out more hay and stuffed it into the net across one corner. He was dusting off the bits of grass as Gordy came out of the stall. He got a mischievous expression and dropped a handful of hay bits over Sam's spiked hair.

"Hey!" Sam squealed. "Don't put that crap on me."

Gordy grabbed another handful and shoved it down the back of Sam's shirt. The prickly bits set Sam's back to itching as he yanked his sweatshirt up and tried to shake out the debris. After a moment of irritation, he couldn't help but be affected by Gordy's impish grin.

Sam grabbed hay from the floor and showered it over Gordy. He even got the hay down the front of his shirt. Gordy growled, pawing at the hay covering his head before ripping up his shirt and brushing at his chest. After a few seconds, he narrowed his focus on Sam.

"You little shit! I'll get you now!"

Sam took off for the door. He had no chance of escaping Gordy, but their good-natured fun was making him happier than he had been in a long time. About then, Gordy grabbed his sleeve and spun him to a stop. By now Sam was laughing and enjoying their play. When Gordy got two hands on Sam's shirt, he twisted and slipped out of it.

"There you go, Mister Hot Football Player. Think you can catch me now?"

"Oh, your ass is *so* mine!" Gordy lunged at Sam, throwing his shirt to one side. Sam yelped and dodged, narrowly missing Gordy's attack. He spun again, but Gordy's years

45

of catching fleeing quarterbacks played to his advantage. Gordy wrapped his rough arms around Sam's chest, and in the next instant, they landed on the hay-buried barn floor. Gordy pinned Sam's face as he rolled on top.

"Got you, you butthole!" Gordy said with a deep chuckle.

Sam tasted the tint of bile in the back of his throat and the tightening in his chest.

"Gordy, get off. Get off me."

"Oh no, not until you admit I am the undeniable winner for all time."

Sam fought to keep the panic under control, but when Gordy shifted his weight, trapping Sam under him, the fear surged forward. "Get off. I mean it, Gordy. Get off me! I can't breathe."

"What's the matter? Do you not like being tackled? Make me move. You can do it."

Sam lost the last shreds of his control. Flashbacks filled him and Gordy's pleasant heat became something else. He screamed. "Get off me! Get off me *now*! You're *not* going to do it again! I won't let you. I *won't*." Sam's emotions were in tatters and hot tears rolled down his cheeks.

Gordy flew off, kneeling beside him. "Sam? You okay, man? Sorry. I thought we were fooling around." Gordy reached down to help Sam.

"Don't touch me. Give me a minute. Please," Sam said as he tried not to hyperventilate. A few seconds passed and Sam got to his knees, pressing his forehead against the ground, then eased himself to his feet. He glanced over to Gordy, who was pacing back and forth like a hyperactive kid.

"What happened? I thought we were just goofing around. I didn't mean to hurt you."

Sam shook his head, coming to a decision. "You didn't hurt me, but I have a few — emotional landmines." He met Gordy's panicked eyes. "Let's go into the trailer. I don't want to discuss what happened while we are in the barn."

"Okay, whatever you say."

Sam frowned as he led the way. In complete silence, Sam sat down while Gordy dug in the fridge for a moment and poured him a glass of orange juice. He disappeared into the bedroom and came back pulling on a T-shirt and handed Sam a jersey.

"This isn't a conversation to have without shirts."

Sam nodded. "Probably a good idea." He caught Gordy's gaze. "You don't know me very well. You sure you want to have this discussion? We're likely to be in the too-much-information zone."

"You're a good guy, Sam. If you want someone to listen, I'm willing to be that person. If we're going to hang out, it would probably be good if I understood better."

Sam nodded as his heart pounded faster. He ran his tongue over his parched lips and tried to gather his thoughts. This was going to be difficult. He took a drink of his orange juice then stared at his hands. "I had something happen in high school. It makes it hard for me to do some stuff."

Gordy stared at him for a moment before shaking his head. "I'm trying to not be stupid here, but I'm not following."

Sam shook, moisture gathering at the corners of his eyes. "This is hard—really hard."

"It's okay to tell me. I swear it won't change anything."

"This will change everything." Sam's laugh had a brittle edge. His stomach roiled as he thought through how he would explain.

"I was assaulted in high school. It fucked up my head. If people get too close or start touching me, I can't take it. Someone trapping me? Well, you saw how I lost my shit."

Gordy watched him for a minute, a frown growing on his face before he asked the question Sam dreaded. "What did they do to you, Sam? What happened?"

Sam's laughter had a sharp edge to it. "I was raped, Gordy. Three guys from the football team. They held me down and raped me. Took turns." Sam wrapped his arms around himself. He thought Gordy started to try to comfort him and shuddered. But Gordy clenched his fingers onto the table and didn't move. It was a minute before either of them spoke.

"That's horrible," Gordy said with a pained expression.

"I've only told a few people. But it seems to keep affecting what we do. I've been going to the counseling services office for a while and some things are improving, but" — he turned to Gordy, needing to clear the air between them — "you're a nice guy and have been patient when I've went off."

"I'm not sure what to say, Sam. I'm glad you felt safe to tell me, even though we haven't known each other that long."

"You've been understanding through all the crisis moments and the whole gay thing. It had to be weird for you."

Gordy fell silent, dropping his gaze and avoiding looking at Sam. After a few moments, Sam let out his held breath. "I read it all wrong, didn't I? Hey, I'm sorry about freaking you out with my garbage. I'll get my stuff and — "

Gordy reached across the table and squeezed Sam's hand. When their eyes met, it surprised Sam to find a fearful expression. He lifted a brow as he tried to puzzle out what was wrong. Before Sam could say anything further, Gordy started talking.

"I guess we both have our secrets. Mine have been hidden for a long time and I need to tell someone. Someone to talk to, you know? It's personal. I'd appreciate it if you'd keep it between the two of us. I know it doesn't seem like that big of a deal to you, but it's a huge thing for me."

Sam frowned, uncertain where this conversation was going. But Gordy seemed to be building to something important. "Tell me, Gordy. I promise it will just be between the two of us."

Gordy took a deep breath and blurted out. "I'm gay."

Sam sat stunned for a moment before he leaned forward. "You're gay?"

The dam seemed to have burst for Gordy as it spilled

out. "Yes, I'm gay. I like dudes. I'm not sure why I thought this was the right time to talk about it and you were the right person to tell. I do think what happened to you was horrible. Oh God. I'm not trying to grandstand. It just came bubbling out. Only a few friends know. Sorry to fall apart like this."

Sam couldn't help but shake his head and chuckle. "Seems like we both have a shitload of things we're dealing with. It's not a competition. I've told you about all my issues — well, as much as I want to talk about them right now. But you —"

"This isn't something new. I've known I liked guys since before high school. Football scholarships paid for tuition and the side jobs like tutoring help with the bills. I've heard too many derogatory comments made about gay guys over the years."

"You're coming out is your decision. I would never out you. I promise."

Gordy nodded then smiled at Sam. "That was the reason for all the stammering and stuttering when you told me you were gay. I wanted to tell you then, but I was afraid."

Sam grinned. "It's all good. It'll help keep the weirdness from the conversation now that we know each other better."

Gordy patted Sam's hand and smiled. "We better get back to homework. I have a bunch due before Thanksgiving."

Sam shrugged. "I have to work on Black Friday. And dark gray Saturday. And pale red Sunday."

Gordy chuckled. "Yeah, I have to take care of the wheatgrass steers. The undergrad research assistant gets the crap assignments, so I'm here all weekend, too. It looks like turkey and dressing TV dinner for the holiday." He considered Sam for a minute before continuing. "Since we're both stuck here, do you want to come out and have Thanksgiving with me? I'm not a bad cook, but I only know how to make massive quantities of holiday food."

Sam grinned and licked his lips. "Turkey and dressing?"

"Yup. Turkey and dressing, mashed potatoes, gravy…the

works."

Sam considered for a moment before breaking into a grin. "I could bring pumpkin pie. Don't worry. I'll buy it."

"You bet. Pies are good."

Chapter Seven

A gust of wind caused the metal siding of Gordy's trailer to crackle, and ice pellets popped against the tiny kitchen window. It distracted him, but a few seconds later he refocused on the food they had been cooking all morning. He hadn't expected to enjoy the meal that much. But Sam was relaxed, and they'd enjoyed their time together.

Sam glanced up from the corner chair and Gordy grinned at him. "We made enough to feed about ten people. I hope you're hungry."

"Starved. I've been drooling since I got here. It smells delicious."

Gordy filled the table until he had to put the last platters on the counter. He poured them each a glass of tea and sat across from Sam. "Did I miss anything?"

Sam chuckled. "I can't imagine what you might have forgot. You were right. You have enough food to feed my whole dorm floor."

"Want to invite them?" Gordy asked, enjoying the feelings of satisfaction washing through him. He considered Sam a close friend.

"No! They can find their own man who wants to cook for them. They can't have mine." There was an awkward pause and Sam flushed.

Gordy dismissed his comment with a wave of his hand. "No worries. I enjoy cooking for someone who likes my food. Dig in."

After Gordy emptied his third plate, they slowed down. By the time Sam finished his last plate, he was stuffed. He stretched and groaned.

"That was delicious. I ate way too much."

Gordy burped then grinned at Sam. "Excuse me. I'm stuffed." He glanced around before meeting Sam's gaze. "You want dessert? That pie you brought looks delicious."

Sam groaned and grabbed his stomach. "If I eat anything else, I'll pop. Let me help clean up and take care of everything. Dinner can settle then we can see if we want pie."

"Sounds like a plan." They put the food away, although they had eaten much of what Gordy prepared. After he shoved the last container of leftovers into the fridge, he glanced outside before turning toward Sam.

"Seems to be snowing a little. You can stay in here and keep warm. It won't take me long to feed and water the animals."

Sam grinned and rubbed his stomach. "Sitting around here won't help work off all the food I ate." He wriggled his way from behind the table and put on his hoodie. As he zipped up the light jacket, Gordy chewed the inside of his lip. Sam noticed Gordy's quizzical expression. "What's wrong?"

Gordy glanced outside to the now-blowing snow then back to Sam. "It's windy. I have a heavy work coat you can use. I might have worn it twice, but I swear I didn't get anything on it."

Sam glanced out to see white flakes falling sideways. There was a moment's hesitation before Sam nodded. "Yeah, I'll take you up on that offer. It seems like it's colder than when I got here."

Gordy opened a small closet and pulled out a reddish-brown coat that appeared—and felt—like canvas. Sam tugged it on, closed the zipper and laughed. The coat came almost to his knees and the sleeves hid his hands, like a kid wearing his dad's clothes. He cracked up laughing.

"Well, at least it'll be warm, even if you look like a little kid," Gordy said.

Sam flapped his arms for a moment before he stopped

teasing Gordy and rolled up the sleeves. Soon they were out the door with Sam headed for the stable and Gordy for the barn with a fifty-pound bale in each hand. A few well-practiced maneuvers and Gordy had the animals fed and ready for the coming storm.

It relieved Gordy that Sam didn't come to the barn to help. Last time's disaster was fresh on his mind. The wind screamed past him, and he secured the coat collar tightly around his neck. As he made his way through the pens, Sam raced to the trailer. Gordy couldn't help but chuckle. *He looks like a kid playing dress-up in adult clothes.* But the wind carried tiny drops of rain and Gordy found he was much more interested in reaching the house rather than speculating about Sam. By the time he made it into the trailer, he found Sam curled up with Gordy's coat around him like a thick blanket.

"Damn, it's cold out there," said Sam.

Gordy rubbed his hands together to get some warmth into them before taking off his coveralls and tossing them onto his bed. The heat of the room soaked into him as he put a few plates on the counter. He glanced over to find Sam watching him and smiled. "I thought it was time for dessert. A piece of pumpkin pie with whipped cream?"

Sam grinned but didn't turn down the offered sweets. Gordy handed him the filled plate and dropped into the other seat with a huge portion of pie covered in a mound of whipped cream. He ran his spoon into the pile and was lifting the huge piece to his lips when he saw Sam's smirking face.

"What?" Gordy asked.

"Do you like a little pie with your whipped cream?"

Gordy's eyes twinkled as he popped the spoonful into his mouth and munched. Once he'd swallowed the bite, he answered, "I don't know what you're talking about."

Sam giggled. The second he did, he cringed. It was a giggle.

Gordy found it cute and endearing. He ducked his head

and didn't make eye contact. He didn't want to embarrass Sam any further. Gordy enjoyed spending time with Sam. More and more, their time together was pleasant and relaxing. He wasn't going to spoil the moment. It was too good. The quiet stretched out as the last of their meal disappeared.

Sam leaned back and grinned. "Not bad homemade pie. What do you think?"

"Yeah, and you did such a good job boxing it and putting the fancy design on the crust."

"Nothing but the best for my football buddy."

A pleasant warmth washed over Gordy at Sam's words. He'd never allowed himself to be close to anyone until he'd met his best friend, Nate. Not that he didn't have other friends, but he had a connection with Sam he'd never experienced before. He'd always considered Sam handsome, but his bravery in the middle of all the crap he was dealing with seemed admirable. He was startled to realize Sam was watching him.

Sam held out his empty plate and grinned. "How about another piece of delicious pie?"

Gordy grinned and took the dish. "No problem, boss." The knife flashed a few times before Gordy gave them each another helping. Gordy stood with one hip against the counter as he ate. He turned to slip his plate in the sink when he peered outside. The trees made low creaking noises and were coated with a thick layer of shimmering ice. "Crap! Looks like we're having a heck of an ice storm."

Sam slid off the seat and moved beside Gordy. He watched for a minute and his face twisted. "I better go now before it gets worse."

"I don't know. It seems bad already. You might want to stay."

"It'll be fine. I'll take it easy."

Gordy questioned Sam's choice, but he seemed determined to leave, regardless. He frowned a little. "Take my coat with you, in case something happens and you're stuck in the car."

Sam considered for a minute before he nodded. "Okay. That'd probably be a good idea." He gathered a few things and headed for the door. Sam grabbed the handle and pushed, but nothing moved. He turned to Gordy. "What's up with the door?"

Uncertain what was wrong, Gordy grabbed the knob and pushed. Nothing moved for him, either, and he was afraid he knew what was wrong. This time, when he twisted the handle and threw his weight against the door, it popped open to a crystalline landscape.

It stunned Gordy. Everything had an ice coating. Tree branches bent under the weight until they touched the ground. The rain wasn't lessening either. He turned to Sam. "You're not going to make it to campus. It's bad. It's not safe to drive back tonight. You can stay here. When do you report for work tomorrow?"

Sam peered through the open door in time for an overloaded branch to snap with an explosion filling the yard. He frowned and turned to Gordy. "It's not safe to drive, but where would I sleep? If I can get to campus—"

Gordy interrupted. "Don't be crazy. I can take you into town tomorrow morning after some of the ice melts. The four-wheel drive will handle it better than your little beetle bug." He motioned to the dark house a few yards away. "The Clarks are gone for the weekend and I don't have a key to the house." He shot Sam a grin. "It seems they don't trust college students with the keys."

Sam rolled his eyes. "Figures. Faculty are such weird-ass people." He glanced around the trailer. "Where would I sleep?"

"The table makes into a bed. It drops to the seat and the cushions rearrange."

"Looks like you're stuck." He glanced around. "What do you want to do?"

Gordy opened a drawer, brought out a new deck of cards and tossed them to Sam. "Ever played Spit?"

* * * *

Sam woke with a shiver. The room was pitch black — not the regular darkness of night. This was different. He couldn't see anything. A few seconds later, the cold had him shivering.

"Sam?"

It comforted him. At least he wasn't spinning off into one of his night terrors. "Gordy? Why is it so dark? And so cold. I'm freezing."

"We lost power. The heater doesn't work without electricity."

A flashlight clicked on and illuminated the trailer. Even in the minimal light, Sam could tell Gordy was down to his briefs. Not that Sam was wearing much more, he'd left on his T-shirt and underwear. Gordy pulled out another blanket and motioned to Sam.

"Come on. You'll freeze. We can share my bed and help keep each other warm. We can pile all the blankets I have on top of us and we should be fine. There isn't another source of heat."

Sam hesitated, unsure of what he wanted to do. A strong gust hit the trailer and freezing air curled close. He pulled the blanket tight and scooted to the edge of the bed. Gordy flicked the flashlight toward him and he hoped he didn't look as panicked as he felt. Gordy dashed that hope with his next words. "I promise. No funny stuff. But the closer we get, the warmer we'll be."

Sam's teeth chattered, and he made a decision. "Okay. I'm freezing. If we can keep warmer huddled in the bed, then let's get our shit moved."

"Give me your blanket and hold the light for me. I'll get the extra quilts from storage." He gave Sam a grin. "The equipment shrinkage is so bad that I couldn't find the goods if I had to."

Sam couldn't help chuckling but tossed Gordy the bedding he'd had and took the flashlight. It only took a minute or two before he was motioning Sam. "Get in. Dang, it's cold."

Sam shot forward, crawled to the far side of the bed and wriggled under the blankets. He watched Gordy slip in beside him and work the bedding to cover them. He turned so they faced each other. "We need to get close. Tell me what you want to do."

Sam nodded and swallowed hard before he shook his head. "What if we spoon together?"

"Works for me. Who's the little spoon?"

Sam chuckled at the visual. "What if I'm the big spoon?"

Gordy flipped to his side and scooted closer to the middle of the bed. "Start spooning, I'm freezing."

Sam nodded and steeled himself. He scooted across the bed until their skin pressed together. After a few minutes, he'd warmed enough to stop shivering. That's when he trembled for reasons other than the cold.

"Get closer. I'm freezing." Gordy reached for Sam's hand, pulled his arm around and held it against the middle of his chest. Sam inhaled sharply, and his senses filled with Gordy's scent. He braced for a reaction, but instead felt a warmth curl through him. A few minutes later, Sam was warm and content before slipping back asleep.

* * * *

Sam woke with a sigh as they shifted. He ran his hand over Gordy's chest, enjoying the heat and textures of his body while the two of them became more and more awake. He pressed himself tight and ground his cock against Gordy's hard ass. Sam was so rigid that his cock ached. With only two thin layers of cloth between them, Sam's erection slipped between the cheeks of Gordy's muscular butt. A soft groan filled the room—Sam froze.

Now, wide awake, Sam considered his options. There was a part of him that wanted to hide, gibbering, in a dark corner. But he was in charge. He was the one controlling the situation. Another part of him wanted to rip off what few clothes they were wearing and fuck Gordy's round ass. He pressed his hands lower, circling the fan of hair on Gordy's flat stomach. The tips of his fingers slipped along the top of Gordy's briefs and Sam wanted more.

"You go any farther and you have to make breakfast afterward." A soft chuckle filled the room.

Sam's fantasy shut down quicker than if he'd had a bucket of ice water dumped over him. He jerked away from Gordy, uncertain of anything other than he missed the heat he'd left. Gordy turned until they faced each other. It surprised Sam that the only emotion he could see from Gordy was concern. "You okay? It's nothing to freak out about. Boners happen, you know."

Sam grinned at the bad pun and took a minute to study the man lying beside him. Gordy had a thick covering of morning stubble and Sam wanted to rub his hands over it. His lips were full and called to him. His dark nipples were hard. A thin line of hair gathered in the center of Gordy's torso and traveled downward until it disappeared under the blanket. Mesmerized by the sight, Sam let himself be drawn to Gordy. The linebacker seemed to feel the attraction, too, and moved to close the distance.

Their lips touched and fire oozed through Sam. His cock throbbed and flexed inside his underwear. Gordy cupped his head in one hand as they pressed their lips together. He ran his hand over Gordy's chest, rubbing his thumbs over the hard nipples. Gordy groaned into Sam's mouth as their kiss continued. A few minutes passed as Sam's lust for his tutor grew. He pushed forward until he had Gordy on his back and Sam lay across him, grinding against Gordy's hip. He reached lower, the tips of his fingers slipping inside Gordy's briefs when he gripped Sam's wrists.

"Sam. I think we should cuddle and smooch for a little longer. This is nice, and I want it to end as good as it started."

Sam sighed but slipped his hands from Gordy's underwear. He leaned over and kissed Gordy again. "You're right. I want it to end on a good note, too. Besides, it's still cold here."

Sam pressed Gordy onto his back and lay on top. He kissed down Gordy's neck and soon had him groaning and making small thrusts upward. Their confined shafts rubbed together. With another hard kiss that ended with a playful nip on Gordy's bottom lip, Sam laid his head in the middle of Gordy's broad chest and sighed. A few minutes later he realized Gordy was still making little squirming motions and panting. The air became laden with a now-familiar masculine scent and the spice was delicious. He inhaled deeply, filling himself with Gordy's musk. It surprised Sam when Gordy lifted him off and to the side.

"Sorry, Sam. It was great. But a few more minutes and I'll lose it."

Sam felt a sense of peace and playfulness. He coiled downward and flicked his tongue over Gordy's nipple then bit at it.

Gordy growled through gritted teeth and jumped from the bed. Sam admired the almost-naked body before him. His briefs were wet where the tip of his hard cock had been trapped. Gordy's dick flexed again and clear pre-cum oozed through the fabric. The combination left nothing to the imagination as Gordy stood there, his briefs tented. He tried to adjust himself, but failed miserably. He looked down to Sam's smirk.

"It's funny, huh?"

Sam chuckled. "Maybe a little."

Gordy reached down and ripped the blankets off Sam, who yelped and rolled onto his stomach. His cock was so hard that he had to arch his groin off the bed. Gordy reached out to slap his ass but hesitated then dropped his hand. But the grin never diminished.

"Yeah, big boy. I'm going to take a shower. We at least have hot water for a little while. And it'll be quick." He smirked at Sam. "The towels are in the shelves just outside the door in case you need one." In a final move, Gordy stripped his briefs, tossed them beside Sam and left the room.

Chapter Eight

Someone knocked as Sam moved around the room to dress after his shower. His weekend with Gordy had become more fun than Sam had expected, but neither of them seemed ready to talk about waking up together. It impressed Sam that Gordy had been good to his word. He'd chauffeured him to work and just about everywhere else, until Sunday when they restored the power and the branches were cleared from the roads. The previous couple of days he had heard nothing, but both of them had finals coming soon. Gordy also said the last game of the season was in a few days, so he was preparing. A text from Gordy inviting him for pizza surprised Sam.

The pounding resumed at the door, startling Sam back to his present state of nudity. "Hang on. Hang on. Don't get your knickers in a knot." He found a pair of pants clean enough to wear, slipped them on and tugged the zipper closed before opening the door. Rachel stood grinning at him. "About time, slow poke. You said we'd go to lunch. I don't think you're following the dress code. Get a shirt on. And I'm staying right here. Otherwise, you'll fall back asleep."

Sam opened his closet and grabbed one of the few shirts left. He slipped into it and buttoned up. She waved her hand in front of him. "It's December. We're going Christmas shopping. Remember?"

"Okay, okay. I'd forgotten. Let me grab a coat." He looked for a minute before spotting the coat Gordy'd loaned him hanging behind the door. Sam smiled and tugged it on. The hint of musk drifted to Sam as he zipped it shut. He glanced to Rachel with a grin. "Ready."

Rachel stared at him for a moment and lifted an eyebrow. "Did you go to Goodwill or something? Where'd you find that thing?"

Sam ran his hand over the outside of it and couldn't keep from grinning.

"Oh. My. God. You got laid by the football player."

Heat flashed over Sam at the accusation, along with a tightening in his chest. But he scowled at his friend. "I did not get laid by Gordy. You're letting your imagination run away. I'm not the one with fantasies about jocks."

"Yeah, I'm not buying it. You still have that 'I got lucky' glow."

"Geez! Let it go. I'm hungry. Come on."

An hour later, Sam was full and following Rachel on her Christmas trek. More accurately, he was playing Sherpa as she added bag after bag to the pile he was carrying. They passed yet another specialty shop decorated in all shades of pink. "I can get my sister's present here. I swear, I'm almost finished."

Sam waved her on and started toward the seating. "Go ahead. I'll wait right over here."

She disappeared into the sea of pink as Sam lowered himself to the bench with a sigh. He sat for a few minutes before glancing around. He couldn't help but notice the outdoor store opposite him. Curious, he gathered up the bags he was carrying and made his way inside. The skintight clothing on ripped mannequins drew him closer. He was staring at the end counter filled with shirts of all the popular colors when Rachel found him.

"Did you get lost? You know the name of this store is not what they sell?"

Sam looked at her and rolled his eyes. "I know what they sell. I was just…"

Rachel studied him for a moment then her eyes twinkled. "You're buying something for the boyfriend."

"He's not my boyfriend, even if he is—" Sam stopped,

realizing he was about to out Gordy. "It's just a nice gesture. He's helping me pass my bio class."

"Nice? Hmm. Interesting."

"Shut up and help me pick out a color and size."

She turned to the display and flipped through the ones at the bottom before pulling out a black and gray compression shirt. She tossed it to Sam. "There. He'll like that one."

Sam held out the shirt then glanced at Rachel. "It looks huge."

"That his coat?"

Sam swallowed hard but nodded.

"Then it will fit just fine, and you'll get to drool over him."

"He's just a friend that—"

"And how is *my* gift coming along?" Rachel interrupted Sam.

He grimaced and headed for the checkout.

* * * *

Gordy was chatting as he changed clothes. He and Sam had gotten in the habit of eating together a few times a week. Tonight had been Sam's pick, and Gordy wasn't too sure about the choice. The idea of Ethiopian didn't make his taste buds sing with anticipation. Actually, Gordy had no idea what it would taste like. He'd never had it. He wasn't sure how to explain it. It didn't sound good.

"This is where you want to go? You can always change your mind," he said.

"Gordy, you've never tried Ethiopian. Why are you so against it?"

"I'm not sure. It sounds like a place where they serve fried crickets as appetizers."

Sam chuckled and made shooing motions with his hands. "Come on. Don't be such a hick. Get dressed. I made reservations. If it wasn't good, they wouldn't require reservations."

Gordy walked to the door as he smoothed his clothes with

his hands. "I bet it means there are a lot of people around here trying to impress their friends."

Sam shrugged. "You could be right. But it's my turn and we're going to eat something other than burgers and cheese fries." Then Sam turned back and said, "No. You can't order from the kids' menu. It won't kill you to eat something that isn't breaded and fried."

"Hey!" Gordy protested. "I'm not that bad. I like just about everything."

"Get dressed. You'll like this, too."

With a little quiet grumbling, Gordy took a final glance at his clothes and headed for the pickup with Sam just behind him. They were halfway to the restaurant when Gordy turned to Sam. "If this isn't good…"

Sam grinned. "If you don't like it, you get to pick for the rest of the month."

Gordy grinned and relaxed. He was fairly certain he was going to be picking where they ate for a long time. They parked, made their way to the entrance and Gordy opened the door. Delicious aromas washed over him, and he was practically drooling before they were seated.

Less than an hour later a stuffed Gordy sat opposite Sam. Sam had been right. He'd liked the food. The soft flatbread was a great meal all by itself.

Gordy waved a last piece of bread at Sam. "This stuff is delicious."

"The injera?"

"Yeah, so good." Gordy popped the last bite into his mouth and closed his eyes as he savored it. After a few additional sounds of Gordy's approval, Sam chuckled at the linebacker.

"For someone who didn't think he would like the food, you seem to have enjoyed it."

"You were right. I'll admit it. It was delicious." Gordy decided this was a good time to give Sam his gift. He reached into his pocket, pulled out an envelope then slid it across the table.

Sam picked up the unmarked white envelope and turned to Gordy. "What's this?"

"Just something I want you to try. You know, like a new food."

Sam tapped it on the table and lifted an eyebrow at Gordy. "I think I've been hustled. What's in here?"

"Open it and see. It won't bite. You might even enjoy it."

Sam tore open the end of the envelope and peered inside. He tilted it back and forth for a minute before Gordy became impatient. "Would you pull it out already?"

Sam tilted the envelope to his mouth, sent a puff of air inside then turned it upside down. A length of stiff paper slid out onto the table. Sam studied it for a minute before looking at Gordy.

"A ticket to the game tomorrow?"

"Yeah. You said you've never been and you're graduating in May, so this is the last game of your college career."

Sam fidgeted, turning the ticket over and over in his hand. "Gordy, I'm not sure. I'm not a big fan of sports. I—"

Gordy cut him short, not wanting Sam to work out a way to avoid going. "It's close to the fifty-yard line behind the players. I knew you wouldn't like sitting in the student section. Those guys get crazy."

Sam sucked air through his nose, refusing to meet Gordy's gaze. "I'm not sure. It doesn't seem like a great idea."

"Come on. It's only a few hours. It can't be the worst thing you've sat through since you started college."

Sam chuckled and shook his head. "No, I'm sure that's true. But, a whole football game? I don't know anything about football."

Gordy detected he was weakening. "You can pick where we eat for the rest of the month."

Sam grinned and slapped the ticket against his palm. "No complaints?"

"None."

Sam sighed. "Get me a foam finger."

* * * *

Sam leaned against the seat as the crowd roared again. He understood more about the game. It amazed him how crazy all these thousands of fans were. Gordy had been right. His seat was close enough to talk with the players. Gordy shot him a smile when the team first came out. From that point on, Gordy's focus had been on the game and nothing else. Sam had to admit, Gordy was good. He'd done a little homework on football and realized Gordy's role as tackle was one of the toughest. But, at least today, he was stopping anything they put up against him.

But now they were down to the final few seconds of the game and were behind by three points. Sam fidgeted. It surprised him that he was this wrapped up in the sport.

"Come on, Gordy! Take 'em down!" Sam yelled.

The quarterback called the play and a mass of players sprinted into action. The quarterback dropped back to pass as the linemen fought to protect him. Suddenly one of the opponent's players broke through, and the quarterback fumbled the ball.

A moan rippled across the stadium and Sam stood with everyone. He sensed a shift in the players and Gordy popped out of a crush of men. He grabbed the football, tucked it under his arm and sprinted for the goalposts.

Everyone in the stands was screaming madly, including Sam. The crowd cheered Gordy on as players from the other team tried to run him down. Sam screamed himself hoarse, and a few seconds later, Gordy vaulted over the final attempt to stop him and ran into the end zone.

The stadium erupted.

Sam let himself be swept onto the field with the flood of fans and the rest of the team. He cheered at the members of the team carrying Gordy amid the celebration. He dimly knew the students were tearing down the goal post. A few minutes passed and university police cleared the field. Someone grabbed Sam, and he turned to find Gordy holding his arm.

"Meet me outside the locker room. Okay?"

"Okay. Sure."

"Great! I want to celebrate."

The next hour passed in a rush. Several people gave him a questioning look, but nothing more. He tried to stay out of the way, not wanting to bring too much attention to himself. The crowd thinned until Sam was alone. He wondered if Gordy had forgotten him or had been pulled into another celebration with his teammates. He checked his watch again and was close to deciding Gordy had already left.

"Did you think I wasn't coming?"

Sam turned and beamed. Before he thought it through, he jumped into Gordy's arms, and kissed him. "Congratulations! That was an amazing play. You won the freaking game."

Panic flooded Gordy's face, and he scanned the area as he lowered Sam to his feet. "Hey, we've gotta be careful. We don't want anyone to see us."

Sam nodded, giving him time to verify no one was close. It took a minute, but then Gordy's tensions seemed to melt away. And once they did, he grabbed Sam in a tight embrace, pressed his face hard against Sam's neck and gave him a quick peck on the cheek. Sam held onto Gordy and inhaled. The sharp aroma of soap underlying Gordy's scent was something Sam found he looked forward to each time they were together. He grinned that a smell he'd found so objectionable a short time ago had become one of his favorite things. They stood for several minutes enjoying their time together before Gordy took a step back, letting Sam's hand drop into his.

"I guess we should get going. I'm starved," Gordy said.

Sam squeezed the hand that enveloped his and grinned. "And where would the conquering hero like to celebrate tonight?"

Gordy chuckled and bumped against Sam's hip. "I don't get to pick until after break. That was the deal, remember?"

"Well, I'm instituting the 'Saved the Day' rule. The person who saves the day gets whatever he wants."

Gordy curled his arm around Sam's waist. "Oh really? Anything?"

Sam wiggled his eyebrows at Gordy, enjoying the playful banter between them. "Anything you think you can handle."

"Hmm, I think I can handle just about anything you got."

"You think so, stud?"

The sound of a door closing destroyed their fun. Gordy dropped his hands and stepped back. Sam ached at the action, but understood Gordy was trying to figure out how to deal with coming out and when. Sometimes you worked with what you got. Unfortunately, Gordy hadn't gotten the same set of cards as he had.

A few seconds later they heard the sound of footsteps down the concrete ramp to the locker room. A man came into view and Sam couldn't help but cringe. The guy looked like a televangelist lacking any conscience. He steeled himself and stood his ground. Gordy seemed concerned enough that Sam moved closer for moral support.

"Hey, Coach," Gordy said.

The guy nodded toward Gordy. "Great job, Hager. Spectacular play today. Saved the game."

Gordy's cheeks turned crimson. "Thanks, Coach. I appreciate that."

The coach turned to Sam. "Hi, son. I'm Coach Miller."

He held out his hand, and it was all Sam could do to keep the revulsion from his face. He took the offered hand and gave a firm shake. "Sam Doherty, sir. I'm a friend of Gordy's. He's been tutoring me in biology so I thought I'd see a game."

The sweep of Miller's eyes made Sam's skin crawl. While still staring at Sam, he said, "Good job again today, Hager. Keep up your guard, though. Always keep up your guard."

"Sure, Coach. I'll keep watch."

The man formed his fingers into a gun and pointed it at

Sam. "Good to meet you, kid. Don't get Gordy into any trouble."

Sam nodded, but kept silent. The guy flashed his far-too-perfect teeth in a smile with all the authentic warmth of an iceberg. He studied the man as he disappeared into the parking structure then turned back to find Gordy's enthusiasm undiminished.

"Let's swing by the house," Gordy said. "I can put on something other than sweats then we'll grab dinner."

Sam slapped Gordy's shoulder and grinned at the excitement. "Sounds good. In your honor, we should have either steak or barbecue."

Gordy sprinted toward his pickup. Sam settled back while Gordy did a recap of the game on the drive to the trailer, most of which Sam didn't understand. He nodded a lot and uttered the occasional affirmative, which seemed to be enough to keep Gordy going. Sam was dissecting what the coach had said and trying to decide what part had been aimed at him. Deep down, his biggest fear was that he'd seen them being affectionate, and Gordy would get the backlash.

"Here we are! Won't take me but a minute." Gordy bounded out of the seat and was in the trailer before it registered with Sam that they'd arrived. He followed Gordy inside, closed the door and sat down to listen. He also planned to enjoy the scenery while Gordy changed clothes.

Gordy stripped off his skintight shirt and tossed it into the laundry. He ran a towel over his chest and Sam licked his lips at the sight of the rippling hair. His scent grew stronger as he moved like a caged animal. "Can you believe it? Can you? It fell right into my hands."

The heat rose in Sam as Gordy pulled down his sweat pants and kicked them off. With Gordy stripped to his jockstrap, Sam breathed heavier. He swallowed hard and smiled at Gordy. "It was amazing. You were fast, too. You saved the day for State."

Gordy came closer and retrieved a beer from the fridge. He dropped onto the seat next to Sam and drank several swallows. As he did, he stretched his arm up and exposed the thick growth of damp hair that filled the muscle-bound cavity. The smell was sharper, more intense. Sam leaned closer, unable to resist, and he inhaled. Gordy's smell filled him and his cock hardened and grew down his leg. He was long past any kind of civil behavior.

He realized what he was doing and froze, his whole demeanor changing in the hope he hadn't been discovered. But when he lifted his gaze, Gordy's twinkling eyes were all he needed to see. Gordy had caught him, but he hadn't wanted to startle Sam. Feeling a little like the rabbit cornered by the wolf, he wasn't certain what to do next.

"It's okay. I thought you didn't like the — natural me."

Sam swallowed hard again. "My opinion seems to have changed. You smell...good."

Sam felt a little trapped with Gordy so close, but Gordy didn't move as his smile grew. As the tension slipped from the situation, Gordy spoke. "Do whatever turns you on. Tell me what to do."

"Really? You'll let me order you around?"

"Sure. It sounds fun."

Sam scooted a little closer, grinned and leaned forward. He paused only a few inches from Gordy's thickly furred armpits and couldn't help but inhale again. The smells spun about him and Sam's cock hardened until it was a throbbing ache between his legs. Unable to resist any further, he pressed his face into the damp pit and grabbed Gordy's bicep. With his face buried, Sam enjoyed the feel of hard muscle under his touch. He shifted sideways, flicking his tongue over Gordy's nipple and a sigh rewarded his effort.

Sam pressed Gordy against the seat and climbed onto him. As he moved in for a kiss, Gordy suddenly tensed. Sam panicked when he pushed from under Sam and regained his feet. He sprinted to the bedroom, cursing the entire length of the house. "Damn it. Damn it. Damn it!"

Shock flooded Sam as he recoiled from Gordy's reaction. He straightened his clothes and worked out what happened as Gordy yanked on clothing. Then he heard it, the frantic honking of multiple car horns. It was still faint but unmistakable. He leaned over to the window and peered outside just as one huge pickup slid to a stop in front of Gordy's trailer. The doors swung open and two enormous men grabbed the truck's roof, stood in the doorway, and yelled out. "Gordy! Gordy my man! Gordy the hero!"

The door to the bedroom slammed open and Gordy shot out, trying to pull on his second boot. As he stumbled around, a second and third vehicle appeared, he glanced at Sam with a sigh. "It's the team, at least some of them. They want to celebrate."

The din outside grew in volume while Sam tried to think. Gordy frowned as he stepped to the door. "Knock it off, you animals! This isn't Joe's! Keep it down."

"Come on, Gordy! We want to parrr-teee!"

Gordy spun toward Sam. "Come with me. Please. They aren't bad, just excited."

Sam glanced out the door to the scene of adult men behaving like twelve-year-old boys. He was surprise to find that he didn't have any animosity to them, but since he was half their size, he might be an easy target.

As if he could read Sam's thoughts, Gordy said, "They won't dog you. I promise. Or they'll answer to me."

"What are you going to tell them? That you want to have the guy you tutor in biology along for fun?"

Gordy slumped against the door and looked crestfallen, but he refused to admit the difficulty of the situation. The determination was clear as he met Sam's gaze. "You should come. They don't have to know we're more than friends."

"Maybe later, Gordy. You deserve to celebrate with the team tonight."

Gordy's face twisted and he let out the breath he was holding. "I would. And we were working on an outstanding celebration before they arrived."

Sam fought the urge to caress Gordy a last time, but instead smiled and popped his fist against Gordy's shoulder. "That'll be for sometime later. But for now, how are you going to explain me being here?"

Chapter Nine

Gordy staggered into the locker room and dropped to a bench. Every muscle he had was sore and sweat drenched his clothes. After sitting for a few minutes, he peeled off the workout shirt he was wearing and dropped it to the ground. He was trying to tug off the shorts that had adhered to his thighs when someone else walked in and sat beside him.

"Damn, Gordy. Why is Coach so pissed at you?"

Gordy glanced up to Nate's concerned face. He shook his head and tried not to sigh. "Damned if I understand it. He's been kicking my ass for the past few days. I'm so sore it's not even funny."

As he stripped, he moaned, then started toward the showers. He heard footsteps behind him and looked back to see Nate had followed him. He hung his towel outside the door, went inside then turned on the water as hot as he could stand. Nate moved to the same set of nozzles and rinsed off. After a few minutes, Gordy's pain lessened and he soaped up. By the time he'd covered every sweat-crusted part of his body, he seemed more human.

"You should soak in the sauna. It'll help."

Gordy shook his head. "Finals are coming up and I need to study. Thank God, we'll have a break from practice. I'm kind of glad we didn't make it to a bowl game. Maybe it'll give Miller time to get over whatever he's pissed at me about."

Nate got a wicked expression on his face and Gordy cringed. Nothing good happened when that expression arrived. "So, how's the tutoring going? It must be intense if he had to come out to your place right after you won the freaking game."

Gordy couldn't keep himself from scanning the shower and was relieved to find them alone. He turned back to Nate, wondering how to handle the situation. "Hey, yeah. He's struggling in biology."

"That's funny. I thought the guy you were tutoring was a complete ass, although a hot one. But wasn't that him in the free ticket section, too?"

Gordy panicked. Nate and his wife were the only ones who knew he was gay. Nate had been his freshman roommate and he'd been fine with it. But he also loved to make Gordy squirm.

Nate grabbed his bottle of soap and squirted it over Gordy's chest, catching him by surprise while Nate's deep laughter filled the room. "Relax, man. I was just yanking your chain. Besides, I got your back. Always remember that. I don't care if you do have the hots over a cute redhead."

Gordy stood under the hot spray, staring at Nate. Once the heat worked its way into his stiff muscles he let out a sigh of relief as he washed the soap off his body. "We've been getting along pretty well, and he seemed to enjoy the game. But I've never been in a relationship before so everything is kind of confusing."

He glanced over as Nate wiped the water from his face. He grinned at Gordy. "Did he reward his stud man for saving the game? I'd have tried to talk Sarah into it."

"Jeez! Too much information. And you don't need to know about my sex life."

There was a moment of quiet before Nate continued, "But I'm serious, dude. Whatever you need, I'm here for you."

Gordy had a few minutes while washing off the soap before he had to deal with the offer Nate had left hanging. The last of the white suds disappeared down the drain and he turned off the shower to discover Nate standing at the doorway, toweling off. He grinned at Gordy, who prepared himself. But it seemed his friend had moved on to new topics. "You going home for the break? Practice starts the day after Christmas. Sarah isn't happy about it. But then she isn't pleased with me right now in general."

Gordy grinned at his friend and his unending litany of marital drama. But it left Gordy wondering about his break as Nate vented on his current issues.

* * * *

Sam slid his car beside Gordy's pickup, leaped from his car and ran toward Gordy's trailer. He skidded to a stop at the door and pounded. "Gordy! Hey, Gordy! It's Sam. I have to show you something."

The door popped open and Gordy stood in the doorway in only a pair of workout shorts and flip-flops. "Hey, Sam. Get in here. It's freezing."

He scrambled up the steps, closing the door behind him. Sam slipped into his seat while Gordy went back to whatever he was cooking. Gordy was always cooking. But he was also hungry all the time. Sam was shaking with excitement from his news when Gordy turned to him.

"What's up? Didn't you have work or something?"

Sam vibrated with nervous energy as he shook the paper he held. "No, they changed my schedule. Finals week. But look! Feast your eyes on this."

Gordy wiped his hands on a towel and took the sheets of paper from Sam. As he read down the page, his smile widened. By the time he turned to Sam, the smile covered his face. "You got a B in the class. A freakin' B! That's fantastic."

Giddy with excitement, he pointed at the score on the top. "See that? Did you see what I got on my final? Ninety-two! I was flunking this damn class, and now I made a ninety-two on the final."

Gordy lunged forward and grabbed Sam in a hug. Sam tensed at first, but then found comfort in Gordy's embrace. The heat and scent of Gordy's bare chest swirled in the surrounding air. Gordy said in his ear. "That's fantastic,

Sam. I'm so proud of you."

Sam wrapped his arms around Gordy and squeezed tightly. He couldn't recall being this comfortable in someone's arms in a long time. Then he realized his hug had become more of a cuddle and eased himself away. A sense of relief filled him when he saw the smile was as wide as ever across Gordy's face. The food popped in the skillet and Gordy stepped over to take care of it.

"We have to celebrate. I'm taking you out to dinner," said Gordy.

"You're half right. We are celebrating. But you pick the place, and I'm paying for the meal."

"Sounds like a plan."

A short time later found Sam following Gordy to his pickup. The shirt looked good on Gordy, but the jeans made Sam drool. His muscular butt and thick legs were working on Sam like he'd never experienced before. A month ago, Gordy was the antithesis of who he would have wanted to date, now Gordy turned him on in ways that surprised him every day. But he still hadn't brought himself to where there was any real physical contact. Well, beyond a lot of cuddling in front of Gordy's television, but that was only leaving both of them hard and horny. That was the effect it had on him, anyway.

He slammed the truck door shut and grinned at Gordy. "So, Mister Excellent Tutor, where do you want to go? It's all on my tab tonight."

The pickup roared to life, and Gordy backed out of the driveway. He was chewing up gravel road toward town when he turned to Sam. "How about Joe's? We can split cheese fries and burgers."

"Sounds like a plan, but you can have the fries. I'm getting fat."

Gordy chuckled and reached over to pat Sam's flat stomach. "Dude, you're miles from fat. You even have the sex muscles showing."

"Sex muscles? I'm afraid to ask."

"You know. Those muscles on each side that point at your goods." Gordy raised one side of his shirt and ran a finger down his abdomen. "Along here, except I'm too fat. Mine don't show."

Gordy motioned with his hands as he split his attention between Sam and the road. "Go ahead. Pull up your shirt and I'll show you."

Sam grinned and hid his shaking hand as he tugged the side of his shirt up, exposing his torso. Gordy reached over and ran his beefy finger along the crease of muscle and into the top of Sam's pants. For Sam, the touch was erotic, and it was all he could do to keep from moaning and pressing himself against Gordy.

The pickup lurched as they entered the parking lot, and Gordy's touch disappeared as he grabbed the wheel with both hands. They exited the pickup once Gordy parked. Sam tried to hide the sizable bulge in his pants before they reached the streetlights and everyone would know they'd been fooling around. The blast of music and rumble of voices helped him refocus, so by the time the hostess seated them, it wasn't noticeable.

Once they'd ordered a pitcher of beer, Gordy smiled at him again. "That grade is amazing. I might not have been able to bring it up if I'd gotten that low. You kicked it in the ass."

The waitress dropped off the plate of cheese fries and disappeared. Sam grabbed a fry and chewed on it while he considered. "It was you, totally you. I would have failed if it wasn't for your help."

Gordy stabbed his fork into a cluster of fries and stuffed them into his mouth. He chewed for a minute before he swallowed and used his utensil to punctuate his words. "Pretty cool, man. Pretty cool. Now you're done with bio."

Sam played up the drama as he dropped his arms. "Sadly, no. I have to take the second one in the spring. But then I'll graduate from this cowboy school."

"Hey, Gordy! How's it going?"

They glanced over to see Nate cradling a beer in each hand. "Hey, Nate. How's things?" Gordy said.

"Good, good. Just celebrating my last final. How about you?"

"About the same. We were out celebrating Sam's grade in bio."

"Oh, man. I took three times to pass that damn class." He winked at Sam. "I wish I'd had the big lug as a tutor." He glanced between the two of them. "Hey, do you mind if I crash your party? I'm kind of batching it. The wife has a final on Friday."

Sam hid a smile at Gordy's sigh, but Nate seemed oblivious. "Sure, Nate. Pull up a chair. We've been working on an order of cheese fries."

"Cool!" Nate hooked a chair from a neighboring table.

Gordy stared at him for a minute and shook his head. "You couldn't get one glass and then get another? The first beer'll get warm."

"Nope!" Nate tipped the glass to his mouth and chugged it down. It didn't take long before he set the empty glass down on the table. "Damn good!" He ordered a pitcher of beer and another order of cheese fries before turning back to the other two. "What's going on with you two?"

"Just celebrating Sam passing biology," Gordy said.

Nate grabbed Sam's shoulder in a companionable way and squeezed it. "That's right. Great job, man."

Sam tensed, trying to prepare for his unavoidable reaction of panic. Instead, there was nothing. No panic. No sense of suffocation. But also no attraction to this man. Nate seemed like a nice enough guy if a little socially challenged. There was nothing. He glanced over and saw concern on Gordy's face. After deciding to sit back and enjoy the evening, Sam didn't even bother to move Nate's hand. He drank some of his beer and relaxed.

Several hours and more beer than he wanted to consider later, Sam had a nice buzz. "Hey, guys. I'm calling it a night before I'm crawling to the dorm."

Gordy nodded. "I've had enough, too. I can take you home."

Nate emptied their last pitcher into his glass and grinned at the other two. "Weenies! Can't handle your beer."

Sam stood and shook his finger at Gordy when the room seemed to swim. "Whoa! What was that?"

Gordy glanced at him, then stood and grabbed his sleeve. "Let's get you home. You've had enough."

The room wobbled a second time and Sam swallowed hard. "Yeah, big guy. That might be a good idea. Just a fucking great idea."

The next thing Sam knew, Gordy was almost carrying him up the trailer steps. Sam leaned against him while he shut the door. The small light over the sink flipped on and he found himself lost in Gordy's scruffy face. Without thinking, he reached up and caressed his rugged face. "You're fucking good-looking. Did you know that?" Sam waved his hand and chuckled. "Of course you do! Good-looking studs know they're hot."

"Come on, Romeo. You need sleep." He helped Sam to the bedroom and waited for a minute when he realized Sam couldn't undress himself.

"Hold still," he told Sam. "I'll help you get ready for bed."

Sam lifted his arms so Gordy could pull off his shirt. As it cleared his hands, his arms fell around Gordy's neck. Their eyes met and Sam leaned forward until their lips touched. Their heat lit fireworks inside Sam. He trapped Gordy's head and pressed his tongue against his lips. A second later they opened and Sam slipped inside. Gordy met it with an equally passionate kiss. Gordy tasted of beer and his own alluring scent. By the time they separated, Sam's cock was rock hard and he wanted Gordy in the worst kind of way. He kissed down Gordy's neck while he unbuttoned Gordy's jeans. Gordy stiffened then took Sam by the wrists.

"Sam, I can't tell you how much I want to do this, but you're drunk. If we're doing this, you're going to be sober."

Sam tried to grab his crotch again but Gordy stopped him.

"You sleep tonight. I want no regrets. Okay?"

Sam experienced an unsettling combination of disappointment and nausea. Then another wave of nausea washed over him. "Oh, Gordy."

There was soft laughter as Gordy shuttled him to the bathroom. "Come on, lover boy. In a few seconds, you won't be worried about sex."

* * * *

Gordy glanced down the hallway when he heard a low groan. He chuckled and shook his head as he went back to reading his novel. There was rustling in the bedroom and he heard Sam.

"Gordy?"

He set aside the book he was reading and looked over to see a tousled headful of red hair and a cute face scowling at him. "I don't feel good."

"You drank too much last night. You can thank Nate the next time you see him."

"Gordy…"

"Yeah?"

"I seem to remember…uh…something—"

"Nothing happened. You got sick."

"Sorry I acted like an ass. I didn't—"

Gordy waved him off. "Don't sweat it. Everyone has drunken monologues they regret later."

The silence stretched on for several minutes before Sam spoke again. "It wasn't a drunken monologue. I wanted you."

"I refuse to have sex with someone who's drunk, and that especially applies to you."

Sam dropped his chin to the mattress and appeared forlorn. "That's what I was afraid of. No one wants to deal with my junk."

"Nope. You're wrong."

Sam had tears forming in his eyes. "How am I wrong?

Even you don't want to mess with someone as fucked up as me."

"You're wrong for several reasons. First, I won't take advantage of anyone who's had too much to drink. Second, I want to get to know you better. I can't guarantee how it will work out, but I like you." He smiled sheepishly. "Besides, you aren't the only one who has baggage."

Sam started to reply but cringed and lay back on the bed. "Oh God. My head is killing me."

Gordy laid his book on the table, retrieved a few aspirins and a glass of water. His sock-covered feet were silent as he walked to the bedroom door. "Here, take these. Some aspirin should help."

"I might puke."

"It wouldn't be the first time in the last twenty-four hours."

Concern washed across Sam's face, then panic when he glanced under the covers. His voice had a squeak when he turned back to Gordy. "I'm naked."

"It's better this way. Trust me. Your stuff is in the washer. And don't worry, I slept on the couch."

Sam covered his face with his hands. "Oh shit. I can't believe I got sick."

"Well, it wasn't all your fault. I should have warned you that Nate drinks like a fish. No one on the team can compete with him."

Gordy grinned at Sam but said nothing. His stomach growled and Sam's face contorted. Gordy walked back into the kitchen, pulled a bottle of sport drink from the fridge and gave it to Sam. He stared at it for a minute with a questioning look on his face. "Won't this make me puke?"

"Maybe, but I'd guess you're dehydrated. If you can keep it down, you'll feel better."

"What if it makes me sick?"

He sat a plastic trashcan beside the bed. "Try to hit it this time."

Chapter Ten

Gordy paced the floor as he listened to his mother having their typical conversation. Any phone call with his family consisted of a monologue, but he would have liked to get a word in also. It wasn't destined to happen.

"Okay, Mom. Well, you guys have fun. I'm sure you're right. It'll be warmer in Houston than Ardmore." Gordy sighed as he hung up his phone and tossed it to the couch. Disappointment washed over him. He glanced over to see Sam watching him.

"What's wrong?" Sam asked.

"My family. They're oblivious to anyone but themselves."

Sam shrugged. "Most people are. What'd they do?"

"The whole family is going to Houston to my sister's house for Christmas. Her kids are little and she doesn't want to travel. So everyone is driving across the damn state of Texas."

"It sounds like a pain, but you can go, too. Am I missing something?" Sam asked.

Gordy looked even more dejected. "Yeah, one little thing. I have to be back at school the day after Christmas. Practice starts that day and with Coach being an ass, I don't dare skip practice."

"Come home with me. I have to work the day after Christmas, so I have to be back, too. I'm in the same situation. If I'm not back, I don't have a job. It's a huge retail day. And Tulsa is close. We can save gas money."

"I don't think your folks would want a stranger for the holidays," Gordy said.

Sam laughed and shook his head. "Some years, my

parents have an outlaw's Christmas and invite everyone who can't be with their family to our house. It's a blast. So, it won't be a problem."

"I don't know, Sam. I think that's pushing my luck."

Sam pulled out his phone, tapped it a few times then put it to his ear before looking at Gordy. "We can settle this and you won't have to spend the holiday alone in your trailer eating a TV dinner." Before Gordy could argue, Sam's attention went to his phone.

"Hey, Mom. How are you?" He listened, then, "No, there's no problem. I call all the time, not just when something's wrong."

With another long silence, Sam listened again and rolled his eyes at Gordy. "Anyway, Mom, a friend of mine is going to be alone for Christmas and I told him he should come home and spend the holiday with us."

During the quiet Sam's face turned bright red, and he turned away from Gordy. "Yeah, Mom. It's Gordy, the guy who tutored me. Yes, Mom, he managed a miracle."

Gordy chuckled at Sam's expressions. The exchange entertained him more than anything in weeks. Sam's face looked hot enough to fry eggs. He cut his eyes to Gordy then his focus snapped to the phone.

"Mother." Then, "Mother! You'd better not." Again, a pause. "Okay, but remember that I'm the one who will put you in the home when you're old."

Sam took the phone and held it out to Gordy. "She wants to talk to you."

Gordy took it, holding it like a baby skunk. He shot Sam a questioning expression, but Sam just shrugged. He lifted the phone to his ear.

"Hello, this is Gordy."

"Hi, Gordy. This is Carolyn, Sam's mom."

"Yes, ma'am. Nice to visit with you."

"Nice to talk with you, too, Gordy. I wanted to tell you personally that you are welcome in our house."

"Yes, ma'am. Thank you, ma'am."

"And Gordy..."

"Yes, ma'am?"

"Don't hurt my baby. He's had some rough times in the past few years."

A knot formed in Gordy's stomach. He'd hit a sensitive area for Sam. He realized Carolyn was still talking.

"Is there anything special you'd like for the holidays, Gordy? We don't have what most people would consider the traditional Christmas dinner."

Gordy thought for a minute before answering, "Pie? I love pie."

"Any favorites?" she asked.

"Ahh, pecan — and coconut cream."

"Pecan and coconut cream. No problem. I look forward to meeting you next week. We're casual around here, so don't worry about dressing up. Talk to you later."

"Yes, ma'am. Here's Sam."

Gordy held out the phone. His cheeks were still flushed as Sam finished up the call to his mother. Once Sam had closed the connection, he turned to Gordy.

"Sorry. I didn't know she would get so personal. I guess I shouldn't be surprised, but I always am."

Gordy chuckled. "She was fine. Actually, she was fantastic. Now I get homemade pie for Christmas."

"Don't get too excited. It won't be a turkey and dressing kind of holiday. One year, we had tacos. But you can never say Christmas dinner at our house is boring."

"Pie. That's what I'm focused on."

Sam shook his head and grinned. "She makes good pie. I have to agree with that."

* * * *

They turned onto the unassuming residential street with its two-story houses and mature oaks. Gordy's case of nerves had built over the entire hour drive, and now that the destination was close, his stomach was filled with knots.

As Sam wheeled his beetle down the street, Gordy realized one of the houses had two flags, the stars and stripes and the rainbow flag. His gaze darted to other houses in the vicinity and many had smaller versions of the rainbow flag around their entries. He wasn't terribly surprised when Sam turned into the flag-festooned home. He looked at Sam with raised eyebrows.

"A rainbow flag? Is that just for us?"

Sam seemed confused for a few moments before he realized what Gordy was talking about. Then it was Sam's turn to grin. "No, they're up all the time. It's a fairly liberal neighborhood. A few same-sex couples have bought houses in the last few years."

Another thought came to Gordy, but he wasn't certain how he wanted Sam to answer. "Does your family know we're together?"

"No! Absolutely not. You asked me not to tell anyone, and I didn't." In spite of his proclamation, he refused to meet Gordy's gaze.

"But?"

"Well, my mother might have figured it out. If she did, I think she'd tell Dad. Mark probably won't know. But, regardless, everyone is eager to meet you."

"Great."

Gordy truly wasn't sure if he was relieved or upset. Before the conversation could go any further, a crowd of people started boiling from the house. The welcome crew consisted of several folks who had to be related to Sam as they displayed their Irish heritage plainly. From his dad, who Sam favored with his auburn hair and slender body, to his mother, whose strawberry-blonde hair was at the other end of the spectrum, he followed the family traits. The third redhead had to be Sam's brother Mark, and attached to one of his arms was a white-blonde girl whose skin was a match for the others in the family. The last person was an anomaly who seemed comfortable with the rest of the bunch in spite of his Mediterranean features. After hugs and handshakes were distributed, Sam set about repeating introductions to make certain Gordy had met all of them.

"Gordy, let me introduce you to the herd. This is my mom, Carolyn, and my dad, Tom. This whole mess is their fault."

Gordy exchanged a firm handshake with Sam's dad then got a huge hug from his mother. Sam continued with the remaining people.

"The guy who is almost as good-looking as I am is my little brother, Mark, and the Nordic beauty who puts up with him is Megan."

Gordy was a little surprised to get hugs from both of them, but it left him with a warm feeling. But Sam wasn't finished.

"This is Ahmad, who is the last member of the family."

The darker-skinned man shook Gordy's hand and winked at him,

"Yes, I'm from the Lebanese side of the family. You know...Southern Irish." The family all laughed politely before he continued. "Actually, I work with Doug and he and his family are kind enough have me over on holidays when I can't get back to see my family in Michigan."

There was a moment of silence before Carolyn took over. "Supper's ready. Let's get at it before it gets cold."

They settled around the table and started passing the food. Various dishes were packed onto the tabletop until Gordy began to wonder. He leaned to Sam. "Does your family have their big meal on Christmas Eve?"

Sam grinned at him. "No, this is Mom's idea of a light dinner. Wait until tomorrow. She'll knock your socks off. But make sure you get your precious pie tonight. She doesn't make more of those."

She wagged a finger at him. "Now, Samuel Evan. You don't know that for sure. I might have more pies hidden away for Gordy."

Mark leaned in. "Ohh, you got almost the whole name. You're on thin ice."

Carolyn shook her head at them. "You better eat before

Gordy and I get everything." She winked at Gordy."

At that point, the teasing came to a stop as everyone finished filling their plates and started enjoying the good food. Sam had been right. The mix of dishes was different. He was glad Sam had introduced him to all the new foods over the past months. But everything was good, and it didn't take long for Gordy to stuff himself.

Sam's dad groaned, pushed back from the table and rubbed his stomach. "Oh my gosh. That was delicious. Best meal I've had in a long time."

Gordy nodded in agreement. "It was amazing, Mrs. Doherty. The pies were wonderful."

"Glad you liked it, Gordy, because I'm sending enough with you and Sam to keep you fed for a week. And please, call me Carolyn. Mrs. Doherty is Tom's mother." Her smile welcomed Gordy. The group all sat appearing content for a few minutes then Sam's mother motioned them into action.

"All right, who's helping clean up? Then we can all relax." The family swung into an obviously well-practiced routine. They soon had everything back where it needed to be, and the dishwasher humming as it cleaned the first load. They all made their way to the living room where pillows and blankets appeared from storage. It didn't take long before it sounded as if everyone was asleep. About the time he reached that conclusion, someone shook him.

"You asleep?" Sam asked.

"Nope."

"Come on. We can go to my room and play video games... or something."

"There better not be any 'something' happening, young man."

They both turned to see Sam's mother looking at them through half-closed eyes, but she smiled. When they lay still too long, she motioned them to go on. They went down the hallway to Sam's room.

Sam opened a bedroom door, and with a glance inside, there was no doubt it was his. Every square inch of desk and screens, televisions and other electronics covered the walls. Controllers and remotes spread out everywhere. It was obvious Sam enjoyed his toys. He'd shoved his bed and one small table into a corner. Otherwise, it was an unremarkable room. Even with the abundance of computers and video games, Gordy found it similar to the rooms of guys their age — even some older than he and Sam.

There was movement in the hallway as Mark and his girlfriend entered the bedroom next to them. Gordy grinned as Mark closed the door with an almost inaudible click. He turned to Sam with the smile still covering his face. "Will your parents let them stay in his room with the door closed? Mine would have a cow."

Sam shrugged. "Once we started college, they said the keep the door open rule was over. But don't be fooled. They also said they don't want to hear anything going on. And my mother has amazing ears. If she hears them, she'll be knocking on Mark's door."

Gordy shook his head. "If it's all the same to you, let's leave your door open. I don't want to know that your mother can hear us making out."

Sam chuckled and pulled Gordy in for a quick kiss. "I promise, no moaning. It's bad enough to hear her knock on Mark's door. "

Gordy helped Sam set up one of the units and soon they enjoyed blowing up everything that crossed their virtual path. After they'd been playing for a few minutes, Sam turned up the volume. When Gordy shot him a questioning look, he leaned close and whispered, "Mark owes me."

Gordy chuckled as they went back to their play. The game soon drew them in and they lost track of time until Carolyn was at the door. Sam turned down the sound. "Your dad and I are going to bed. If you'd keep the noise down, we'd appreciate it. Don't stay up too late. I want us all to have breakfast and open presents together."

"Sure, Mom. We won't be up much more than an hour. Tomorrow morning will come bright and early."

"Thanks. Enjoy your night."

She started to leave, then reached over and closed his door. Gordy grinned at Sam. "I love your mom."

They went back to the game they were playing, but as the evening wound down, Sam glanced at the clocks with more frequency. They reached a good stopping point and Gordy paused the game. He stretched and yawned. "I'm tired. Your family parties hard. I'll need rest to keep up with everybody tomorrow."

Sam looked a little sheepish. "Sorry, but since I told her we'd be done in an hour—"

Gordy grabbed Sam by the back of the neck and brought him in for a quick kiss. "I'm tired, Sam. It sounds like a good idea to get some rest. Since you open presents on Christmas day, I bet things start early."

Sam flushed a little but managed a smile. "Early enough. It was ridiculously early when we were kids. Then Mom and Dad said we couldn't get out of bed until six. We'd lay there and watch the minutes tick off."

"I understand. We'd open everything Christmas Eve, but Santa came and filled our stockings. We had to wait for the parental units and they never got up before seven. I swear they'd lie around in bed and make us wait."

Sam nodded and laughed, but Gordy glanced around the room. After a minute, Sam became concerned. "What's wrong?"

"Where did you want me to sleep? With all the Christmas stuff, I doubt your parents want me in the living room."

Sam stammered for a minute before getting out his explanation. "I guess I thought you'd sleep with me. Is that okay?"

Gordy's eyebrows shot upward. "Sam, I don't want to upset your parents. I can sleep on the floor. I don't think it'd be a good idea to sleep together."

"Gordy, honest. They don't care. We're adults, as far as they're concerned."

"You've had guys sleep over before?"

Sam's face turned deep red and his gaze dropped to the floor. "I haven't been with anyone since high school. I haven't…"

Gordy stepped closer, unsure if Sam would want to be touched or not. Deciding to err on the side of trying to comfort him, Gordy wrapped his arms around Sam and held him. "Sorry, Sam. I didn't mean to make you feel bad. What a dumbass move."

He enjoyed Sam's face buried against his chest. There were no tears, no trembling. Gordy got the impression Sam wanted to be held.

Then Sam whispered, "I'm sorry I'm such a mess. I'm not sure why you put up with me. I'm so fucked up."

Gordy tilted his head and kissed Sam on the neck. "You aren't a mess. You're just dealing with some stuff. It isn't like I'm a great boyfriend."

Sam pulled back and stared at Gordy until the silence grew too long. He swallowed hard but never broke their gaze. Sam tensed as he asked, "We're boyfriends?"

Gordy froze for a moment, recalling what he'd said. He'd let the words slip through him and they felt right. He wasn't sure when it had happened, but they'd become boyfriends at some point. Gordy turned to Sam. "Yeah, I think we are. What we were talking about when we first got here started me thinking. You're officially my boyfriend." Gordy spun to Sam. "Is that okay?"

Sam's face flushed red, and he was speechless. He stared at Gordy until he brought the smaller man close and held him tight. Sam shook in his arms. "Sorry, Sam. I didn't mean to ruin the holiday. I feel bad."

Sam made a noise halfway between choking and a laugh. "You didn't ruin the holiday. You just made it the best one I've ever had."

Gordy held Sam tighter and whispered into his ear. "Let's get ready for bed. This will be a great Christmas."

Somehow their acknowledgment that they were more than just friends made everything more sensual for Gordy.

He enjoyed watching Sam strip to his underwear and get ready for bed. His pale skin and ginger hair excited Gordy. The bulge in his briefs did nothing to lessen the tension, either. He realized Sam was in the bathroom brushing his teeth, and he'd stood gawking the entire time. He took off his shirt and was unbuttoning his jeans when Sam walked back into the bedroom. Gordy folded his clothes and laid them across the chair. He had an odd sensation and found Sam staring at him.

"Do you see anything you like?" Gordy asked with a wink.

Sam dropped his gaze and a crimson stain crawled across his neck and face. "Sorry. This is all new to me."

Gordy closed the distance between them and cupped Sam's face. He leaned close and planted a soft kiss. He blew into his ear and slipped his hand across Sam's stomach, through the ginger treasure trail that disappeared into his briefs. There was no longer any question about Sam being aroused as his erection strained against his underwear. Sam gasped for air by the time Gordy had chewed on his ear.

"Mark! Knock it off."

Gordy and Sam shot away from each other as Sam's brother grumbled a reply to his parents. A minute or so later, Sam gave him a sheepish smile. "I guess it's time for bed. Lots of stuff tomorrow."

Gordy drank in the figure before him. He wasn't sure how this would go down tonight, but he didn't want Sam's parents knocking at the door. They weren't bluffing. They fumbled around for a few minutes before settling into the bed with their backs toward one another. They both knew if they started cuddling, it would change to something more intimate.

Gordy reached over and patted Sam on the hip. "Night, sexy."

A noise that sounded a lot like a giggle came from Sam. "Night, handsome."

Chapter Eleven

Sam woke the next morning with Gordy's arms wrapped around him as the two of them cuddled. For an instant he tensed, but a wave of contentment filled him, and he relaxed to nestle back into the warm cocoon he and Gordy had created.

Gordy groaned and stretched before caressing Sam's chest. Sam enjoyed comfort he'd never experienced before. When Gordy traced lower and toyed with the small patch of hair around his navel, he couldn't suppress a sigh.

"Merry Christmas, Sam." Gordy kissed the back of his neck and let his hands rest on Sam's stomach. Sam pressed backward and the rough texture of a hairy chest sent ripples of pleasure through him. He relished the moment, but sighed as he turned to Gordy. "I'd love to spend the day in bed with you, but we better get up before the others are pounding on the door."

Gordy let out a theatrical sigh. "I suppose. This whole adult thing kind of sucks." He leaned in until his lips were against Sam's ear. "My dick's so hard it hurts."

Sam sighed but did the opposite of what he wanted to do. He moved away from Gordy and climbed out of bed. He glanced back to find an obviously aroused Gordy.

"Get up. Whatever we were about to do wouldn't be quiet."

Gordy chuckled and followed Sam. He swatted Sam on the hip as he ducked into the bathroom, and the sting sent chills running through his system. He enjoyed the sight of the man in front of him as he stripped.

"Crap. What're you doing?"

"I'm going to shower. Want to join me?"

The invitation tempted Sam but sanity prevailed. "You're evil."

"Maybe a little, but you'll be missing a lot of fun."

Sam drooled at the sight of Gordy's muscular butt disappearing into the steam. *Yeah, I have a pretty good idea what would happen.*

Instead of following Gordy into the shower, which was what he wanted to do, he found some comfortable clothes that would hide his bulging problem. He decided a tight pair of compression shorts and some loose sweatpants was the best chance he had. He was putting on his T-shirt when the water turned off, and Gordy came into the room, drying himself.

Sam wanted to watch, but he decided more temptation was the last thing he needed. With his back turned to Gordy, he tugged on a pair of socks. The surrounding air thickened as Gordy walked beside him and pulled out clothes. The mix of musk and soap had Sam looking as if he had a joint of steel pipe running along the top of his thigh. As Gordy put on his compression shorts, he chuckled at Sam.

"If you go to breakfast looking like that, your parents will think we were fooling around."

Sam glared at him for a minute then smirked as he turned to Gordy's bag of clothes. Gordy lifted an eyebrow as Sam dug inside and brought out a carefully folded orange and black sweatshirt. Sam pulled it over his head and it dropped almost to his knees. "That should hide anything that's going on inside my undies."

Before Gordy could do anything, they heard Sam's mother call from the kitchen, "Breakfast is ready. Remember, no presents get opened until after everyone finishes theirs."

Sam was the first one through the door and grinned at the pile of food covering the entire table, from the platter full of pancakes to biscuits and gravy and any other breakfast food imaginable. His mother had outdone herself. She brought in the last of the food and motioned everyone to their chairs. "Sit. Eat. There's plenty for everyone."

"There's plenty for everyone on the block," Tom said around a mouth full of pancakes and syrup.

The room filled with chuckles and serious eating began. When Sam glanced toward Gordy, he smiled at the filled plate. Gordy would be his mother's favorite. It wasn't too long before they were all pleasantly stuffed. Sam understood the routine and stood to help clear the table. He grinned to himself when Gordy jumped from his seat and moved to help, too. With so many people assisting, it took only a few minutes to put everything away, and everyone drifted into the living room.

They settled into place as Mark and Sam distributed presents. Soon gifts buried the family members. Gordy and Mark's girlfriend had several, too. Ahmad was at another friend's house this morning, but even then there were a few small gifts for when he returned. Starting with Sam's parents, they worked around the room until it was Sam's turn. He opened the gifts from his family but was anxious to see what Gordy had found for him. He worried the gift might be embarrassing, but that didn't seem like Gordy. But if there was a sex toy in the box, he would die.

He tore into the wrapping paper, only to reveal a plain brown box. He glanced at Gordy and got a nod and a grin. He shrugged, popped open the lid and breathed a sigh of relief. The box contained a deep orange canvas backpack and a card. Sam grinned as he lifted the present and showed everyone. His initials were embroidered on it. It was the perfect gift. He opened the envelope and knew his problems were coming. On the front was a hot guy, covered only by the giant snowflake hiding his crotch.

This time when he glanced at Gordy the expression on his face was pure devilry. Sam knew this wouldn't get less embarrassing. Relieved a nude photo of Gordy didn't slide out, he read the card.

You like looking at my ass so much, wait until we get home and you get your other present.

The heat flashed over Sam's face and neck as he hid the card back into the envelope and under the book bag in the box and closed the lid. He looked up, knowing he hadn't fooled anyone.

"Come on, big brother. Let us read the card. It's just a Christmas card."

Sam tried to find a reply that would wipe the smirk off Mark's face, but his mother interceded before he could.

"Hush, Mark. Megan might have something personal for you, too. Don't tease your brother or it might come back to bite you."

Both Mark and Megan's faces turned bright red, and neither seemed in the mood to tease Sam any further. But he turned to Gordy with a lifted eyebrow. "Your turn, cowboy." He gave Gordy a smile that suggested whatever was in the box would even things up.

Gordy eased the package open and tried to peer inside for clues. The package's dimension said it was a piece of clothing, but Gordy was moving as if the contents were dangerous. After his careful perusal, he finished opening the box to find the compression shirt Sam had bought weeks before. Gordy opened it to show everyone and when he did something fell out and hit the box. Gordy lifted the small clear packet and stared at it. He shook it a few more times before turning back to Sam, who was embarrassed enough to combust. *He doesn't know what they are. Oh shit. Please, God, don't let anyone else in my family know what they are.*

Gordy studied them before looking at Sam again. "Magnetic steel balls?"

Sam motioned for the package of four metal balls. "I'll explain later. Give them to me and I'll put them with the rest of our stuff."

Sam thought he'd gotten through without dying from embarrassment when Megan squealed, "Oh! I know what those are. They're magnetic nipple balls!"

A second later, she realized what she'd said and slapped her hand over her mouth.

* * * *

"How long before everyone forgets what happened this morning?" Gordy asked as they drove down a residential street. Sam and Gordy had escaped as soon as they'd finished Christmas dinner. The laughter over the morning's present had lasted for far longer than Gordy would have liked, but he was glad he wasn't Megan. She'd left right after they'd finished opening gifts.

Sam shook his head and glanced at Gordy. "When the six of us are dead. But by then the story will have been passed to the kids. I can't believe you didn't know what they were."

"Hell no. I had no clue. It's not like I collect sex toys. Why'd you put them in the box? At least mine didn't fall out in front of everyone."

Sam shot Gordy a stern look. "You weren't supposed to shake it out like that. Just hold up the damn box."

"No, you hold up clothes so everyone can see what they look like. It's a rule."

"Where is it a rule? No. Never mind. I don't want to talk about it anymore."

Gordy leaned in and said in his most sultry voice. "You going to show me how to use them when we get back to campus?"

Sam chuckled but didn't reply. But then he turned back to Gordy. "And what's the surprise you have for me at campus?"

Gordy relaxed against the seat of the car and smirked. "You'll have to wait and see. You never know. I might have a baby pig for you or something."

"Great. That's what I need." He glanced at Gordy with a lifted eyebrow.

Gordy chuckled but settled in and viewed the scenery as they drove along. A few minutes later, he turned to Sam.

"Where are we going? You never said."

"To show you my high school." Sam looked a little sheepish but didn't meet his eyes. "I thought it might be interesting. It's sounding a little lame now."

"Nah, it's cool. I like knowing more about where you grew up." They drove into a parking lot for a huge complex of buildings. Gordy let out a long whistle. "This is your high school? That's bigger than the entire town I grew up in."

Sam chuckled as they came to a stop outside the main entrance. They sat for several minutes until the silence got too heavy.

"Did you like it here? I mean, school and all?"

Sam considered for a minute or two before answering. "I came out in high school, during my senior year. I started the Gay-Straight Alliance on campus. You can't be much more out than that."

"Didn't they give you crap? High schoolers can be vicious little sons of a bitches."

Sam pursed his mouth as he remembered the less than pleasant parts of his high school experience. "There was some. It *is* Oklahoma. The bible thumpers believe they have the right to tell you how many ways you're going to hell. Then there are the ignorant rednecks. It wasn't like they could get away with yelling 'fag' at me where anyone could hear, but they pulled shit all the time. That's why I didn't get this car until after high school. They keyed the shit out of the one I drove. The dealership thought I'd taken it into the brush or something."

Sam shrugged as he stumbled upon the memories of his attack. He shook, trying to keep the emotions from bubbling up. Gordy wrapped his powerful arms around Sam and his sensation of safety returned.

"Sorry," Gordy said. "I didn't mean to bring up bad memories."

Sam shrugged again but didn't try to back away.

"It happened in the spring, when they did that? We don't have to talk about it if you don't want to."

"This is about the safest I've felt. I guess you have the power to chase away the bad memories."

Gordy held him tight and kissed his forehead. "I'm here for you and I can tackle the crap out of any bad stuff."

"I haven't told anyone else all that happened. No one. Rachel's got bits and pieces, but I've never told her the whole story."

Gordy's stomach knotted at the idea of helping Sam deal with this part of his life. "Do you want to tell me?"

Sam lifted his head from Gordy's chest and looked at him. The expression on Sam's face worried Gordy, but he prepared himself for whatever might come. Sam shook his head. "I've lost too much to those three already. I'm not dragging us down that path."

He pulled away from Gordy and gave him a kiss. Sam settled back into his seat and stared at the monolithic building in front of him. Gordy was worrying when Sam started to talk. "This place has dominated my life. That ends now." He grinned at Gordy, grabbed his nipple and twisted it. "I'm ready to have fun!"

Gordy jumped then tried to retaliate. But Sam had the car in gear, shot out of the parking lot and onto the street. "Hey, hey. No messing with the driver."

Gordy tried a few more times to even the score but relaxed against the seat and watched the scenery roll past. Gordy was beginning to wonder where they were going when Sam started talking. "I thought we'd drive around and let the meal settle."

"Sounds good. Show me the sights!" And for the next few hours he enjoyed Sam touring him through his version of the town he'd grown up in. Gordy was glad most of these memories were pleasant.

Chapter Twelve

The door popped open and Sam followed Gordy into the trailer. It had been a busy Christmas day. The drive back to campus was quiet, although Gordy seemed pretty excited about something. He had been whistling along to the radio the whole trip. As he sat at the trailer's tiny table, he watched Gordy dancing and humming as he put things away.

"Good grief. Why are you in such a great mood?"

Gordy glanced at him and wiggled his eyebrows. "I still have my present to give you."

Sam's stomach knotted a little. *What does he have in mind? Things were going so well. I hope everything doesn't go to hell.*

Gordy tossed the rest of their stuff into the corner and brought out a small, square box wrapped with rainbow paper. He beamed from ear to ear. Sam shook the box and glanced at Gordy. "What's in it?"

"Open it, goof."

He eased off the paper to find an unmarked box. Sam looked up, filled with both excitement and fear. He opened the package and stared at the content. His stomach flip-flopped, and he pulled out the bit of material. He held it out for Gordy to see.

"A jockstrap? I think it's a little big for me."

"It isn't for you. It's for me to wear" — a smirk grew across his face — "and for you to enjoy taking off me."

The heat rushed up Sam's face, and his cock stiffened. "I bet they'd look good with the nipple things," he offered sheepishly.

"Want to see?"

Sam nodded, unable to speak. Gordy took the jock and disappeared into the bedroom. He surprised Sam by closing the door for the first time. Several minutes passed before it slid open and Gordy stood in the doorway. He wore the new shirt that Sam had bought him for Christmas and a pair of Wranglers that hugged his ass. Their eyes met and Sam had to smile. Gordy seemed more nervous than Sam felt.

"Say something. I'm feeling stupid," Gordy said.

Sam stood and walked closer, ran his hands over Gordy's chest and pressed their lips together. The kiss continued for quite some time, and once they finished, Sam was as hard as he could ever remember. He stood panting at the view of masculinity that stood in front of him.

"You are fucking hot. Smoking. Setting-the-place-on-fire hot," Sam said.

Gordy chuckled. "There. That's what I was hoping for."

Sam ran his hands over Gordy's torso, grabbed his ass and brought them tight against each other. He ground his crotch against Gordy and gave a low growl. "I want to unwrap the package."

Gordy reached down and laid his hand on Sam's crotch and squeezed. "Feels like you're ready."

Sam's heart pounded as he worked Gordy's shirt up to his armpits. He leaned closer and kissed the side of the big man's chest then worked his way over until his lips sealed around Gordy's nipple. He kissed, licked and bit on the hard nub of flesh protruding above the small metal balls until a steady stream of groans came from Gordy. He ran his fingers through the sexy hair on Gordy's chest and stretched so they could kiss again, with more heat than before. A moment later, their kiss broke with a soft sound and Sam smiled.

"How was that?"

Without a word, Gordy took Sam's hand in his and pressed it against the protrusion on his jeans and the hard column of flesh inside it. "What do you think?"

Sam tried to appear serious as he continued caressing Gordy, tugging the nipple toys and swirling the dark hair around his navel. "So, I guess I'll have to work harder to get a passing grade."

Before he replied, Sam popped the magnets off, grabbed a nipple in each hand, twisting and pulling on them while kissing up the side of Gordy's neck. When it seemed that Gordy's groans would rattle the windows, he pushed the shirt over Gordy's head and tossed it to one side. A light scent came from Gordy's body and filled the room. The scent only increased the draw for Sam. As he looked at the almost-naked man he'd been lusting over for months, Sam identified the one thing he needed right now.

He pushed Gordy's arm upward and got willing help from Gordy once he realized what Sam wanted. As he lifted his muscular arm, the aroma almost shoved Sam over the brink. He gathered himself and did what he'd wanted to do for weeks. He pressed his face against Gordy's enormous bicep, kissing and running his tongue over the bulging muscle. Once he'd had his fill of the left side, Sam repeated his performance on the other side. He was purring like a cat by the time he reached his saturation point. He wanted Gordy. Today, things would be different.

Now aggressive, Sam opened Gordy's jeans and tugged them down to his thighs. His cock pressed the fabric outward, ending with a large wet spot. The jockstrap framed his lightly haired ass cheeks. Sam spent several minutes running his hands over every inch of Gordy's exposed body. He knelt in front, pushed his pants down until they pooled around each foot, and Gordy stepped out of them.

Sam enjoyed the sight before him. He'd seen Gordy in various stages of undress on numerous occasions and up close once. But now Gordy's body was inches from him, and he could enjoy it for as long as he wanted. Gordy was huge. He didn't have the physique of a body builder, but his shape displayed a lot of power. Of everything, though,

Sam loved Gordy's butt. The slight texture and its bulging muscular shape left Sam wanting to explore it more. He led Gordy to the bedroom, shoved him backward onto the bed and stripped. In a few seconds, he was undressed and crawling toward Gordy.

Before he could do much of anything, Gordy had run his fingers through Sam's deep red bush and tugged at it. "Damn, you're sexy as hell," Gordy said.

Sam's face flashed hot and his cock flexed, throwing off a clear thread. He gasped and braced himself when Gordy reached between his legs, wrapped his hand around his throbbing dick and squeezed.

Sam felt a familiar sensation and jerked backward. "Oh crap. Don't do that or we'll be done in about ten seconds."

Gordy crawled closer and gave Sam a kiss on the shoulder. "Did you realize this is the first time I've seen you naked? You're a hot dude."

Sam was certain his entire body was flushed red. His dad always called it the curse of the gingers. When he was little, Sam had thought it was funny, but it wasn't as cute in a twenty-two-year-old about to have sex for the first time with a hot guy who didn't turn shades of pink. He realized Gordy was waiting on him.

"It's your call. I want everything to be fantastic for you. So, what do you want?" Gordy asked.

Sam shook, the feelings too much. Where he'd been so certain of himself a few minutes ago, now he wasn't sure about anything. He looked at Gordy, hoping he had ideas.

Gordy smiled and ran his fingertips over Sam's face. The touch built new waves of pleasure. "We can do anything you want, but let's start with the basics."

Sam swallowed and nodded, but was uncertain what Gordy meant. He realized Gordy was crawling across the bed toward him with his stiff cock fighting the confines of the jockstrap Gordy still wore. He took Sam by the ankles, spread his legs, and crawled between them. Gordy kissed up the inside of Sam's thigh while his breath came in gasps. The sensations were close to overwhelming when Gordy stopped, and Sam sighed in disappointment. He lay gasping on the bed while Gordy moved over and pulled out a small box. He reached inside and Sam could guess what he was holding.

"I know we're both tested, but this will cut out any nerves about it."

Sam nodded, still panting for air as Gordy unrolled the condom over Sam's steel-hard cock. Gordy moved back between Sam's legs and flicked his tongue, kissing higher and higher until he was working Sam's ball sac. He lunged forward and took half of Sam's cock in his mouth in one shot. He bobbed his head a few times then came off gasping for breath. "God, you're huge."

Sam blushed again, but before he could say a word, Gordy had plunged downward. It didn't take long before Sam was groaning and thrashing on the bed. He raced to the edge accompanied by that familiar sensation.

"Gordy. Gordy! Fuck!"

Sam's body tensed and trembled. Gordy stopped as the first flash of ecstasy washed through Sam. The ripples of pleasure surged through him again and again as Gordy stroked him. Once the last of his orgasm had oozed out, Sam collapsed against the bed. He panted as Gordy crawled up the mattress beside him and held him tightly in his arms. Gordy caressed Sam's chest and lightly kissed his neck. Sam was enjoying the cuddling when the condom shifted. He turned back to Gordy and kissed his cheek. "I think I better clean up or we'll be washing sheets tonight."

Gordy laughed but reached down and squeezed Sam's dick. He squirmed to escape. "You're not helping. Give me a minute." Sam dashed into the bathroom to get rid of the condom then clean up with a warm washcloth. He popped out of the room to find Gordy lying on the bed with his hard cock stretching the fabric of his jockstrap. Sam moved between his thick legs, caressing and kissing higher and higher. By the time he reached Gordy's crotch, there was a wet spot covering almost a fourth of the pouch.

Sam pulled the waist band down and trapped the column of flesh. He teased along its length until Gordy was squirming on the bed, then he paused. Gordy looked up and cocked his head.

"Something wrong?"

"I don't know how much…"

He sat up and gave Sam's shoulder a gentle squeeze. "We can do whatever you want. Gymnastics and handcuffs can wait a few days."

Sam chuckled, and with an evil glint, snatched the jock off Gordy. He moved closer, rolling and tugging at Gordy's balls with one hand and stroking his shaft with the other. Gordy watched him for a few minutes before closing his eyes with a sigh and laying back. Soon the room filled with soft moans of pleasure as Sam teased Gordy closer to the edge. When he dug his thumb into the underside of Gordy's cock, he thrust upward and groaned. Through gritted teeth, Gordy said, "I'm not going to last much longer if you keep that up."

Sam chuckled and stroked slower. After he had Gordy squirming under his touch, he stopped. "Lube?"

Gordy motioned to the drawer he'd gotten the condom from before collapsing on the bed with his hands thrown over his head. Sam retrieved the bottle and held it out. "Industrial size? Where you afraid you would run out?"

Gordy rose and looked at Sam through half-lidded eyes. "Some of us don't have a couple of inches of foreskin. Cut me some slack."

Sam grinned, rose on his knees and stretched the end of his foreskin. "Jealous?"

"Nope, gives me more things to play with. Now, get back to what you were doing."

Sam drizzled the gel down Gordy's cock and stroked again. Sam worked the full length, twisting his fist to work the sensitive ridge of the crown. Sam was trying to control Gordy's pleasure, who was having none of it. "You better behave."

"Or what?"

Sam grinned then rubbed his lube-coated fingers over the patch of skin under Gordy's balls. Gordy froze for a minute and his cock twitched. A few seconds later, the first cream-colored strand landed on Gordy, clinging to his chest. His moans grew in volume as his cock continued to convulse while Sam rubbed Gordy's sweet spot. As each thick pulse landed, it coated more and more of Gordy's torso. Then the final load leaked out, accompanied with a soft groan.

"Good God, you come in buckets." Sam's statement made Gordy look so uncomfortable that he had to chuckle. "I think you coming buckets was hot. I'm thrilled I got you that excited."

"You did, but I better get cleaned up before the bed's covered."

"Hang on. Let me do it." Sam bounded from the bed, retrieved his damp cloth and wiped off Gordy's smeared chest. A few minutes later—and at least one trip to rinse the cloth—as he wiped up the last spot, Sam leaned down and kissed the center of Gordy's chest.

"Damn. You are incredibly hot, and that was a lot of fun," Sam said.

Gordy took the cloth from him and tossed it in with his dirty clothes. He lay back and pulled the sheet and blanket over him. Sam stood uncomfortably for a moment before Gordy flipped back the covers and smiled. "Are you getting in bed or what?"

Sam's face erupted into a grin that stretched from ear to ear. He crawled across the mattress then curled against Gordy. The texture of Gordy's chest and his warm scent mixed with the smell of sex provided a level of comfort he'd seldom known before. Gordy twitched the bedding closer, brought Sam in tight and kissed the nape of his neck. They fit together like puzzle pieces, and Sam was content.

* * * *

Gordy stood and stretched his muscles that were cramping painfully after sitting unmoving for the past several hours. Sam stared out of the window as Gordy limbered up. He glanced outside to the brown-and-tan landscape and leafless trees that covered the surrounding area. He realized Sam was looking at him and a smirk crept across his face.

"Sorry. I'm getting fried. I need a little break."

Gordy dropped his hands and stretched his neck with a sigh. He leaned against the cabinet in the tiny kitchen. "I've been thinking about something. We've been hardworking college students since Christmas, and now next week is spring break. We deserve a vacation."

Sam crawled across the couch and kissed Gordy on the cheek. A moment later he did it again and the heat engulfed him. It didn't take long before Gordy's desire grew. But he didn't let it get too far before he stopped them. He took Sam's shoulders in his hands and considered his words.

"We've been playing around for months now, and it's been fun. Don't think it wasn't."

"But?" Sam said.

"Well, I don't want to be with anyone else, and I'm tired of condoms."

Sam sat for a minute or so. The silence worried Gordy. "Let's forget I said that. I should keep my mouth shut. Okay, let's move on to something else."

Sam was shaken, seeming on the verge of tears. Gordy moved closer and took Sam in his arms. "Shit. I'm sorry, Sam. I'm such a dumbass sometimes."

Now tears were rolling down Sam's face, and Gordy panicked. He realized Sam was laughing through the tears. He released him enough so their eyes met. "You're laughing?" Gordy asked.

"I hate to be dense, but did you say you wanted us to be exclusive?" Sam asked.

Still confused, Gordy nodded. "Yeah, not using condoms kind of means you are exclusive."

"It also means you don't want to sleep around. You only

want to be with me?"

"Yeah." Gordy blinked.

"So we've moved into the sleeping together, planning things together and sharing our clothes phase. Shit like that?"

Gordy refused to hold back the humor. "Well, I'm pretty sure my clothes would fall off you since I weigh almost twice as much. But, yes, we're into hard-core, serious relationship stuff. I want to spend my free time with you, which brings me to my question. I'd like for us to get tested so we can do away with all the safer sex stuff. That way we can have wild monkey sex on spring break at Purgatory."

Sam looked stunned. So many expressions washed across his face that Gordy thought he might explode. He seemed to focus on Gordy and his smile lit the room. "Absolutely! To everything. I get tested every six months, even though I haven't been with anyone. But another test before the big trip would be fine."

"I get physicals a couple of times a year and you're the first person I've even kissed since high school. But I want to make sure I'm clean before we take the big step."

"The big step, I like that. It sounds long term," Sam said.

"Sounds good, doesn't it?"

Sam almost bounced over to Gordy, grabbed his face and kissed him hard. Gordy's cock hardened from Sam's touch. He let it continue for a few more seconds before easing backward.

"Okay, hang on. Let's wait until after the testing's done and we're at the ski resort."

"We'll never leave our room."

Gordy chuckled and found the thoughts of a week alone with Sam desirable. Right now, they had more pressing issues.

"Come on. We've got to pass midterms or our trip is screwed."

Sam slid his hand lower and squeezed Gordy's crotch but moved away. "Okay. If we have to be virtuous and crap, I can do it. But I'm setting up an appointment with the clinic in the morning."

"Sounds like a good idea. I can't wait. But we have to get our butts in gear or the whole plan is sunk."

Chapter Thirteen

Gordy glanced around the suite, pleased with himself. The room they'd ended up with was huge, with a separate bedroom and a little kitchen. It also had a deck out of a set of sliding doors from the bedroom. This was Gordy's favorite part, since it was the access to the hot tub. The idea of sitting in the tub and watching it snow while enjoying a good beer excited him. The slopes were clearly visible through the huge expanses of glass in both the living room and the bedroom.

"Holy shit, Gordy. This cost you a fortune. We can't stay here."

Gordy smiled. "It didn't cost me much. One of the alumni likes me. He was a tackle when he was in school. Now, he's a big-time donor. So, he told me if I needed a break, it was empty most of the time."

"Well, it's nicer than any place I've ever stayed. When I get a room, I just hope it's clean. This is… Well, I could live here. It's bigger than the trailer."

Gordy opened the refrigerator and found it filled with beer, wine and a few snacks. The freezer had the ingredients for at least two meals. He studied it for a minute before pulling out a package of sirloin steaks and putting them out to thaw. He turned to Sam with a grin.

"It looks like Mister Avery stocked up on things. I spotted a grill on the deck, too, so we can grill them tonight. We can ski a little if you'd like."

Sam hesitated before looking at Gordy. "Well, yeah. Here's the problem."

Gordy laughed. "You can't ski."

"Yeah, that's most of the issue."

He chuckled and shook his head. "I've only been once before and I stunk. Maybe we should sign up for lessons."

"I do at least have the clothes. I found a place online that was clearing out their ski outfits. So, I won't be wearing jeans and a sweatshirt to ski in," Sam said.

They spent the rest of their day in what someone might've loosely called skiing. But truth be known, they spent more time on their butts laughing at each other than doing anything in the realm of the sport. They enjoyed lunch on the hill, but after spending several hours on the slopes, they were ready for a break. The sun had been brilliant all afternoon and Sam's pale complexion was turning a distinctive shade of red. At first Gordy thought it was from exertion, but as he came closer, it became more obvious that Sam had gotten sunburned.

"Oh crap, we need to get you inside so we can put burn ointment on you. You're fried."

Sam glanced at his arms then back at Gordy. "It's winter. There's no way I'm burnt."

"It's been sunny all day, and the snow makes it even brighter. Come on or you'll be miserable for the whole trip." Gordy took off his skis and started to their room. He glanced back to find Sam following, appearing even redder than he had a few minutes earlier. *He'll be miserable if we don't get that taken care of.*

They got into the room and stripped off the layers of clothing they'd been wearing. Sam looked like a cinnamon lollypop. His head and neck were blood red. Gordy held his hand several inches from Sam's face and grimaced. "You're fried. We need to get burn stuff on you, and we need to do it *now*."

Sam seemed somewhat helpless as Gordy rummaged through his bags. Frustrated that he couldn't find the ointment, Gordy caught a glimpse of what he was searching for. He brought out a small flat bag, unzipped it and found the lotion. He shook the bottle and grinned at Sam.

"Off with the shirt. We need to smear this stuff on all the red patches."

Sam eased the shirt to the top of his abdomen and became hesitant. After a moment of silence, Gordy motioned him. "Come on. Take it off. It isn't like I've never seen the goods before. I need to get this stuff on the burns or you'll be miserable."

Sam sighed but pulled the shirt off and dropped it onto the bed beside them. Gordy kept any comments to himself, squirted the lotion onto his palm, and rubbed his hands together. Once his palms were coated, he reached forward and rubbed them over Sam's neck and shoulders. The heat from the burn was undeniable as he coated the mass of freckles across his neck and face. After covering what he could reach, he shook Sam on the shoulder. "Turn around so I can get your front."

Sam sat for a moment unmoving and Gordy tapped him again. "Come on, cutie. Move your little butt."

"Ah, yeah. Hang on a minute, okay?"

Sam tensed under his hands. "What's wrong?"

"Nothing. Just. Well, I enjoyed you rubbing the ointment over me and…"

Gordy tried to work out the puzzle, then realized Sam's predicament and he chuckled. "And you got hard. Stop worrying and turn around. I promise, nothing will happen unless you start it."

A long sigh escaped Sam, and he turned on the bed until he was facing Gordy. He had to admit, the bulge in Sam's pants was impressive. What Gordy would have liked to do was explore the hot ginger sitting a foot away. But then the memories of what Sam had shared came to him and it embarrassed him that he had not kept better control over himself.

"Sorry. I don't seem to have much say over him." Sam tilted his head and studied Gordy. "You aren't helping, either. You make him happy."

Gordy chuckled but a sweet warmth filled him. He

corralled his emotions and focused on coating the rest of Sam's burns. After starting with his neck and face, he slathered the burn cream over the scarlet-colored sections of skin, the heat coming off Sam like a roaring fireplace. He met Sam's half-hooded gaze and smiled. "Close your eyes. Your face looks like a steamed crawdad."

Sam let his eyes flutter shut without challenging Gordy. His hands trembled as he reached for Sam's cheeks. He touched them and coated the burned skin. A small sigh escaped one of them. Gordy wasn't sure who. But the soft scrape of Sam's stubble felt delicious against the tips of his fingers. By the time Gordy had finished, Sam no longer seemed roasted over a bonfire. Gordy leaned forward and kissed the tip of Sam's ear.

"There. You shouldn't be in too bad a shape now."

When Sam turned to him, he was panting and his jeans were tented. Gordy sat back against the headboard and patted the bed between his legs. "Come up here. I want to cuddle."

Sam hesitated for a moment but then grinned and crawled across the bed to Gordy. He slid into the spot and lay against Gordy's chest. He wrapped his arms around Sam and pulled them tight against each other. He drifted his hand lower, teasing at the line of copper-colored hair coming from his khakis. He slipped the tips of his fingers under the waistband and a musky scent drifted around them.

"You smell better than a hot cinnamon roll."

Sam chuckled. "A cinnamon roll? Is that good?"

"A *hot* cinnamon roll. The kind that takes over your nose and you can't think of anything else until you eat it. That's how you are. You take over, and all I want to do is eat you up."

Sam squirmed a little but never moved from his arms. When he slipped his hand out, Gordy caressed Sam as they lay against each other. The alabaster skin gave the sensation of a polished sculpture with the rapid beat of Sam's heart.

He took Sam's hands in his and touched his lips to each palm. He pressed his hands higher, slipping through the red hair on each forearm.

"You're so hot. I want to be with you all the time."

Sam turned in Gordy's arms so they were lying face-to-face and he cupped Gordy's chin, took Gordy's bottom lip between his teeth and tugged. Sam's aggression was exciting Gordy when he lunged forward, pressed his lips hard as he drove his tongue between Gordy's lips and explored his mouth. His body responded, erection growing, nipples turning into hard nubs and his stomach knotting.

Their caresses became more intense with each heartbeat. Gordy rolled them across the bed and sat across Sam's thighs as he stroked his lower body. He wrapped his fingers around the column of flesh in Sam's pants, kneading it as he watched Sam twist beneath him. Gordy slowed then lifted his hands.

"You okay? Do we need to stop?"

Sam panted for a moment longer then his eyes fluttered open. They seemed distant for a second before focusing on Gordy's face. He ran his tongue over his upper lip and swallowed.

"Please. Don't stop."

Gordy opened the top button on Sam's pants and lowered the zipper before slipping from the bed to grab the bottoms and slide them off. He lifted one foot and removed the thick wool sock and kissed the arch of his foot before doing it again on the other side. He studied Sam, stripped down to a small pair of briefs stretched to their limit by the full shaft pressing outward. Sam propped himself up on his elbows and smiled at Gordy.

"Your turn. I want to see the goods."

"Oh? Parading around in front of you for the past four months hasn't been enough?"

Sam said, "Before, it was in that tiny trailer you live in, not a fantastic suite in an amazing resort. Show me that hot ass of yours."

Gordy unbuckled his ski bib, first on one side, then the other and let them fall so they hung from his waist. With the bottom of his compression shirt in his hands, Gordy pulled the tail up and gave Sam a view of his torso. He glanced up to see Sam run his tongue over his upper lip and Gordy smiled as he raised his shirt higher until he exposed the thick hair in his pit. He stood with his hips swaying and smiled when he heard Sam inhale. Gordy popped the shirt off and flipped it across the room before clasping his hands behind his head and exposing his hair-lined armpits.

"You like me like this, all sweaty and funky?"

A sigh escaped Sam that made Gordy's stomach churn and his crotch tighten.

Sam's cock twitched in the stretched underwear and the damp spot marking his engorged knob grew.

Gordy tried to keep the strip going, but had already used up his best material. It wasn't like he knew a lot in this area, and he sure as heck wasn't wearing rip-away pants. Stripper pants took time to get into but if Sam enjoyed watching him strip, he'd give it a shot. He didn't want Sam to be able to say he didn't try. Besides, Sam seemed to be less stressed when they were intimate. So far, they'd had few times like that, but Gordy had no complaints. Just cuddling with Sam made him feel like he was floating. They had time. Gordy was in no rush. He had fallen for Sam.

Gordy realized he'd stopped moving as he'd gotten more wrapped in his thoughts. He flushed and grinned. "Sorry. Zoned out a little."

Sam had an odd expression that left Gordy apprehensive, especially since Sam had lost his erection. But he calmed himself and moved. He would tease Sam until his boner stretched the briefs again. He unzipped the pants, pushed them to his ankles and stepped out of them. He shifted closer and let his hips sway to his imagined music. He traced the shape of his cock and squeezed. The wet spot on the white underwear made them translucent and left nothing to the imagination. He gripped Sam's bare foot and humped against it. It relieved him to see Sam relax and enjoy himself again. A few minutes later, the pressure built, and Gordy pulled back.

Sam opened his eyes and his face twisted in concern. "What's wrong? What did I do?"

Gordy crawled across the bed and gave Sam a light kiss. "You didn't do anything. I was close to coming. You're so fucking hot that I have almost no control." He motioned at the thick length snaking across his crotch. When he leaned in for a second kiss, a tremor ran through Sam. He whispered in Sam's ear. "Wanna see me naked?"

Sam's lip parted and the pink tip of his tongue ran across them as he nodded.

Gordy slipped backward until he was standing at the edge of the huge bed. As he swayed back and forth, he edged his shorts lower and lower, exposing more of his crotch. Once he'd captured his cock, he turned and showed off his ass. He again pushed the stretchy fabric down until it popped below his butt. He continued dancing for a minute or so, showing more of his goods with each wiggle of his hips. His nipples were tingling by the time he bent over, ripped his shorts to his ankles and flicked them across the room. He spread his legs a little wider and peered between them at Sam.

"What do you think?"

Sam chewed at his bottom lip as Gordy rubbed his hands over his butt, giving Sam glimpses of his dusky opening. Gordy's cock was stiff and leaking strands of pre-cum. He heard rustling then Sam caressed his butt with a hot hand. He froze in place, giving Sam the freedom to explore. Gordy sucked in air as Sam wrapped his hand around his ball sac then tugged. A twisting coil of erotic lightning shot through his body and left him tingling.

He turned and moved toward Sam, predatory in his need. Sam's face twisted as Gordy grabbed his underwear and tugged it hard. With a slight ripping noise, they shot lower and with a second tug, Sam's cock slipped out. The column of flesh swung free, leaving a glistening trail across Sam's pale skin.

Gordy crawled higher, kissing across Sam's chest and flicking his tongue over one of his nipples. He moved higher yet, until his face was only inches from Sam's. To his shock, the look on Sam's face was pure distress.

"Sam?"

Sam closed his eyes tight, a tear squeezing out to run down the side of his face. "It's okay. I'm all right. Just give me a minute. I haven't... This isn't..."

Gordy lowered himself as he wrapped his arms around Sam. Their bodies pressed against together as he nuzzled against Sam's neck. He shifted and lay his cheek against Sam's.

"No. Get off! Get off me!" Sam said in barely controlled panic.

Gordy lifted himself to his hands and knees as concern filled him. Before he even spoke, Sam had shot away and yanked a blanket around himself. His breath was coming in gasps. Gordy sat on the bed, not wanting to make the situation worse.

"Sam, what can I do? I didn't mean to trigger anything."

"Not your fault. Oh God. It's hard to breathe."

Gordy moved closer to comfort Sam. Sam's face filled with sheer terror, and he recoiled. Gordy eased away and perched on the edge of the huge bed. When Sam didn't seem to improve after a minute, Gordy gathered his clothes from around the room. Sam's eyes locked on him, but he did nothing to stop Gordy. Once he'd dressed, he met Sam's stare and he'd seemed to calm down.

"I'm sorry. I don't know what caused the panic attack. I couldn't breathe and...well, it wasn't good."

"If it helps, you can have the bedroom and I'll sleep on the couch. But it's early yet, so you can decide later."

The color drained from Sam's face. The expression was one of such terror that Gordy didn't even wait for him to answer. "I'll sleep on the couch. It's a fold-out and bigger than my bed at the trailer." His concern grew as he studied Sam. "Let's relax and watch some TV. I promise nothing will happen. Whenever you're ready for bed, you can have the room to yourself."

A shaken Sam nodded and glanced around. Gordy turned on the TV, sat on the couch and motioned for Sam. "Come sit on the other end and I'll give you a great foot rub."

Sam was hesitant for a moment before giving Gordy a flickering smile, settling on the couch then laying his feet across Gordy's legs.

Chapter Fourteen

Sam was miserable as he leaned against the vehicle door while they drove through the flat, unending country of western Oklahoma. They'd cut the trip short. Sam's episodes were so rampant that the confined cab of Gordy's pickup was closer than he was comfortable with. *This isn't working. I can't be with Gordy. For fuck sake, I can't stand to be around anyone. It's time to cut him loose.* They passed under the interstate and onto the last few deserted miles before they were back at school. It wasn't fair to Gordy. Sam gathered up his courage and ran through what he would say. By the time they'd stopped in front of his dorm building, Sam understood their relationship was ending.

"This isn't working."

Gordy turned to him with a frozen expression on his face. "What's not working? We hit a rough patch. That's all."

"No. It's not your fault, either. I can't be in a relationship. Look how many times we've tried, and the one time we do more, I have a three-day breakdown. It's just not working." Sam's anger grew. It was like a slow boil as the unfairness of the situation overcame him, and Gordy was his target.

Gordy's face became mobile. It looked more like someone had kicked him in the nuts, and he was about to puke. Sam charged onward without pausing. "It's just not working out. I can't keep my shit together when someone gets close. It sucks, but it's the truth. There's no use in drawing this relationship out any further than we already have. It was kicks, but it's time to call it what it is and take the damn thing off life support."

Sam walled away his emotions and met Gordy's stare. By

now, his fury had reached a level where he was no longer reasonable and he wanted Gordy as miserable as he'd made himself over the last few days. As soon as the words had left his mouth, he'd regretted each phrase he'd muttered, but he couldn't seem to keep from throwing their relationship into the bonfire he'd created.

Gordy looked as though someone had ripped open his chest and yanked out his heart. He seemed ready to break down as his lips moved several times with no words coming out. A loud sniffle came from Gordy and Sam was certain a tear rolled down his cheek before he scrubbed his face with his thick flannel sleeve.

"Come on, Sam. I think we're doing okay. Every couple has bad patches. I bet even your parents had rough spots."

Sam folded his arms over his chest and glared at Gordy, as Gordy became the person he hated most. "So, you'd be good telling everyone you are gay and we're doing it? Chance your precious football scholarship to be with me?"

Gordy let out a groan that sounded like he'd just had a three-hundred-pound linebacker hit him in the gut. "You know I... Right now I need..." Gordy had difficulty forming words as he obviously struggled with Sam's statement. Gordy pulled himself together enough to utter one single phrase.

"But I love you."

Sam's heart burst into a million sharp fragments until he wanted to curl into a ball and die. But all the fears and self-incrimination came to a head and exploded with Gordy as the target. "No, you don't, or you'd be willing to give up everything for me. But you can't. Getting your precious degree is all you worry about. I'm just a quick fuck. But then I can't even give you that, can I? You might as well jerk off. Then you don't have to deal with all my fucking drama."

"I don't care. Even if we never have sex, I want to be with you. Don't you get that?"

The last of Sam's nonexistent self-control blew out like

Mount St. Helens and he stooped to a level that would make burning lava and poisonous gas preferable. "That's bullshit. You only want to be with me if I stay in the fucking closet. It worries you more that the damn coaches might find out you like dick. You're afraid if your friends know you're a fudge packer then you won't have anyone but some wimpy boyfriend whose self-esteem is so low he'll let you hide your relationship from everyone."

Gordy's face twisted into a horrifying mixture of pain at too many levels to count. He wiped his sleeve across his eyes as he stared at Sam with his mouth hanging open. Sam jumped out of the pickup and ran to the dorm. What he had done to Gordy horrified Sam. It was like watching the world's most venomous homophobe tear his boyfriend apart, only worse because he'd hit Gordy where it hurt the most.

* * * *

"You look like shit right now. You can talk about whatever your issue is. Just because I'm married doesn't mean I'm clueless about new relationships."

Gordy glanced around his friend's apartment to avoid looking into his eyes. He wasn't in the mood for Nate's home-grown wisdom. It didn't matter if the homespun knowledge came from the depths of Houston. They were from such different backgrounds—the redneck from the sticks and a black kid from the inner city.

But truth be told, neither of them were the stereotype everyone wanted to believe. Gordy had been the scared gay kid and Nate was Gordy's defender and all-around best friend. He was also the only person on the team Gordy had told. His response when Gordy had let it slip was part of the reason they were such good friends. He'd said, '*Cool. Hand me another beer,*' and the controversy never appeared.

He'd also never outed Gordy. The one time Gordy had asked, he'd said, "*It's your story to tell, not mine.*" Nate was the kind of best friend everyone wanted. He'd even been in Nate's wedding — right beside Nate's brother who was the best man.

"Hey, man. What's going on? And don't bullshit me."

"Nathan Wayne, watch your mouth," Sarah said from the kitchen.

Gordy snickered when Nate stuck his tongue out at his wife — but only after he was sure he was out of her sight.

"Brave man."

"I'm not stupid. Nobody wants their wife pissed off." He studied Gordy for a moment and added. "Or husband. Do you want to tell me what's wrong now?"

Gordy slumped against the couch as the days of desolation came crashing back through him. His stomach twisted, and he lost any appetite he had. He tried to hide his feelings but the expression on his friend's face said he'd failed in a big way.

"Come on, Gordy. You've looked like a whipped puppy for the past couple of weeks. What's going on? Sarah and I want to help."

As if conjured by her name, Sarah swept in with a platter in one delicate hand and a bowl in the other. She sat them on the small table in front of the two men just as the aroma reached Gordy's nose. He loved Sarah's spaghetti and meatballs, but today, like so many other times in the recent past, he had no appetite. He gave Sarah a pitiful look, hoping it would buy sympathy for him.

Sarah shook her head of deep red ringlets and frowned at Gordy. "Try a little. Please. I made it because it's your favorite."

"Plus, she knows whatever you leave, I'll eat."

"You hush. I'm talking with Gordy." She turned and focused. One thing he loved about Sarah was you always got her entire attention. This time it left Gordy squirming. Eventually, the overpowering silence compelled Gordy to speak.

"Things just didn't go like I'd hoped. That's all."

"Bullshit!" Nate held up a hand to forestall his wife. "I needed the profanity." He turned back to Gordy. "You haven't looked happy since you got back from spring break. You mope around all day. Even the clueless coaches are noticing. You act like it's all you can do to move. I've been around women on their period who aren't as moody as you are."

He grinned at his wife, who flipped him off. Nate chuckled. "So ladylike. My."

Gordy grinned, too, at least a little. That's why these two were his best friends. Sarah reached over and patted Gordy on the leg. "It's okay to not want to do cartwheels across the library lawn. If you want to talk about it, we're here for you."

Gordy sighed as he played with his food. "What he said hurt…a lot. I thought he'd call and apologize, but I've heard nothing—not a call, not a text, not one fucking thing." He realized what he'd said and grimaced. Sarah lifted an eyebrow but nodded to him.

"Do you want to talk about it? Either way is fine with us." She glanced at Nate and got a nod.

Gordy considered the offer for a minute and realized he wasn't in a good place to talk about their breakup. "No, let's talk about anything else." He dropped his gaze to the floor and shook his head. "Every time I think about it, my gut gets all knotted up, and I want to go to bed and hide under the quilts."

Sarah waved her fork at both of them. "Okay, enough of the sad stuff. Gordy, you'll eat, 'cause otherwise you're never getting my spaghetti and meatballs again. You don't want that to happen." She turned to her husband. "And you, my hot man? You get out the cards and we'll play for a little while once we finished eating. That should help everyone relax."

The two men chuckled, knowing they were defeated. Gordy enjoyed the greatest sense of normalcy he'd experienced since he'd left Colorado.

* * * *

Sam had closed his curtains, so even though it was middle of the afternoon, his room was dark. Rachel sat at the end of his bed and watched him. The sound of her soft breath filled the space until it seemed to roar in Sam's ears. The past few weeks had been among the worst of his life, and it was his own fault.

"Come on, Sammy. You can't just lie around and mope. Get out of bed, eat and go to class." Rachel wrinkled her nose. "And shower. Actually, shower needs to be at the top of the list."

Sam muttered. "Leave me alone so I can sleep." He yanked up the covers and glared at Rachel. "And I don't stink."

"Oh, sweetie, you reek. You're badly in need of time with hot water and soap."

Sam grabbed the edges of his blanket and pulled them around him. As he thought about what he'd done to his life, the gloom of depression threatened to swallow him again. The tears he'd thought he'd exhausted came. He scrubbed his face against the bedding and ignored whatever Rachel had been saying. He rolled himself deeper into the darkness. "Just leave me alone. I've fucked up everything."

"Come on. It's not that bad. You love the big lug, don't you? Didn't he tell you he loved you?"

"It's not that easy. I fucked everything up fifty ways from Sunday. Even if we were together, I'm too screwed up for someone like Gordy."

"Have you tried calling him? It might not be as bad as you think. What if he's waiting for you to apologize? Every couple has problems. You need to give him a chance."

"Not this time. I said horrible, shitty things to him— unforgivable things that should never have been said."

"Well, you know what they say. No one knows your soft spots like someone you love."

"I'm not hungry, Rach. I'm just tired. Let me sleep. I'll be better after some rest."

"No. You said the same thing yesterday…and the day before that…and last week. You will wash that funky smell off, and we're getting something in your stomach besides Pop-Tarts."

Sam brought the blanket tighter around him and ignored his friend. The room became quiet, and he'd hoped Rachel had given up. But instead, the door closed and Rachel was standing on his bed, ripping blankets away.

"Hey! Stop it!" he screeched.

"Get up. You've been doing the gloom and doom thing long enough. I swear if you don't shower, I'll drag you in there myself."

He grabbed at the blankets, but Rachel had already pulled most of them to the floor. A few seconds later all he had left were his briefs and a pillow he wedged in front of his crotch. He glared at Rachel and started to argue when she cut him off.

"Shower. I'll wait in the common room, but if the shower isn't running in a few minutes, I'm coming back in."

His dark mood wasn't changing, but he didn't care enough to battle with Rachel. Once she left the room, he collapsed back onto the bed, unwilling to get up and into the shower. He lay too long and there was pounding at the door.

"Get up! I want water running."

Only his concern that Rachel would carry out her threats had him moving. In a daze, he got his feet on the floor and stripped off his underwear as he stumbled into the bathroom. Sam adjusted the water until it was as hot as he could tolerate. He stepped under the pounding cascade and went through the motions of showering. He managed to soap up and wash his hair, but he didn't care enough to shave, which he normally did in the shower. So, his dark red scruff stayed in place.

He stood with the water streaming over him and his head wedged against the tiles. None of the sensations registered. He was numb and beyond caring. After a few minutes of silent immobility, he turned off the water and toweled himself dry. He wrapped the terrycloth around his waist and made his way back into his room to find Rachel had struck again. She'd laid a change of clothes over a bed that had clean sheets.

Sam shook his head and struggled into the outfit. He zipped up the shorts and slipped his feet into the first pair of flip-flops he found. He took a few halting steps and opened the door to the suite's common room.

Rachel smiled and nodded. "Much better. The beard looks a little mountain man, but I'll take it. Let's get something to eat. I'm starved and I'm sure you are, too."

Sam gave his friend a smile he didn't feel. "Sure, let's get going. I've got all kinds of studying to catch up on."

Rachel grabbed his arm and pulled him to the door. "Okay, we need to eat and not screw around. You're going with me to the rugby game. Laura is playing, and I promised to watch. That means you're making an appearance, too."

She was desperate to help, but nothing had changed. He stood on the edge of a dark place and didn't care which direction he took. The only thing he understood was he'd reached the limit of his endurance.

* * * *

Gordy's phone rang as he sat reading through the most recent assignment in the creative writing class he'd taken on a lark, although it did fill an elective. Gordy would not take classes that didn't count in his degree somewhere. He glanced at the phone's screen. *I don't recognize the number. If it's that important, they can leave a message.* Gordy turned back to struggle through another textbook page. He refused to let his personal life destroy his goals. He would be the first college graduate in his family. He *would* accomplish his goals. At some point, he'd be able to be who he needed to be, but it wasn't now.

His phone buzzed. They'd left a message. *Great. One more*

thing to deal with. He clicked the playback and was shocked to hear Sam's mother.

"Hi, Gordy. This is Carolyn, Sam's mother. I'm sorry to bother you, but we were hoping you'd seen Sam. He hasn't called in several weeks, and his phone just rolls to voice mail. Sam told us you aren't together any more, and we hate to bother you, but we're worried about Sam. He... Well, he hasn't seemed himself lately. I understand this is awkward, but if you see him, please ask him to call us."

"Like hell," he muttered at the phone. He turned it off and tossed it onto the bench seat in his trailer. He went back to his books, trying to focus, but his mind kept going back to Sam. That wasn't like him, but why should he care? Sam had made it very clear he didn't want to be around Gordy any more. *I don't owe him a damn thing. All he left me with was a lot of heartache.*

Gordy tried to concentrate, but after a few minutes, he realized he couldn't remember anything he'd just read. He slammed the dry tome shut and glared at the world. He shoved his sock-covered feet into his boots then stomped them until the floor was reverberating each time his foot struck. Gordy repeated the performance on the other foot and glanced at his clothes. It didn't matter. He looked good enough to find an ex-boyfriend who hadn't regretted ripping his heart out and grinding it into chili meat.

Without a backward glance, he was out the door and roaring down the road in his pickup. He'd already decided he would find Sam sleeping off some Thursday night bar crawl. If that was the drama Sam had shared with everyone else, then he didn't deserve parents who cared whether he was dead or alive. He had a pang of envy for Sam's relationship with his family. If Gordy shared his personal life with his own family? Well, he wouldn't need to worry about getting home to visit on the holidays.

His anger building, Gordy fishtailed a little as he ripped through the parking lot for Sam's dorm. He wheeled into the first empty spot and stalked into the building.

His expression must have been frightful because people dodged from his path as he stomped to door to Sam's suite. His cheeks flushed hot as he tried to think what he'd say to Sam after almost a month of silence.

He reached the nondescript entrance and hammered on it with his fist. The hollow door rattled in its frame with some of the lamination coming loose. A few seconds passed before Gordy was pounding again. The flimsy wood shook even worse until it seemed likely to fall off.

"Good God. Hold on to your panties."

It wasn't Sam, but at least one of his suitemates was sober enough to answer. By the time the few seconds passed that it took for the guy to get to the entry, Gordy's temper flared.

A slit appeared, and Gordy rammed his big body into it. The flimsy security chain broke into three pieces with the middle shooting across the room. The guy who'd opened it stood stunned on the other side as Gordy covered the few feet to bang on Sam's door.

Gordy clenched his jaw as he hammered his fist against the flimsy construction, rattling it. After a second or two with Sam not answering, he drew back to bang on the door again.

"It won't take much for you to knock the door down, but he isn't in there."

Gordy spun to face the guy. "Where is he? His parents called me to see if he was okay."

"Yeah, they called me, too. I have no idea where he is. I haven't seen him all week. He gets in weird funks and we never see him. He'll show up in a day or two."

The total apathy displayed by Sam's roommate left Gordy with a chink in his armor of righteous indignation. "When's the last time you saw him?" Gordy asked as his anger found a new focus. After a moment of contemplation, Gordy got his answer.

"Last weekend, I guess. He was coming in as I was going out to meet friends at the bar." The guy stopped and twisted his lips. "He didn't look good. I told him he looked like shit, but he said he was okay."

Gordy grabbed the doorframe and pulled until it creaked. He took a deep breath as another crack formed in his fury. "Any idea where he might be?"

"His friend's down on the second floor. Rachel might know. Room two-o-two — or something like that."

Gordy rushed out the door before he did something he'd regret. He flew down the stairs as if he were escaping a fire. By the time he reached the second floor, he was breathing harder. Pausing at the landing for a minute, Gordy waited until his breath returned to normal and his temper was under control enough so he didn't want to tear the door down. He stalked through the hall, scanning each room number until he came to the one he was searching for. Gordy tried to calm his warring emotions. He wasn't sure whether he was more worried about Sam or pissed that he was dragged into more drama with the man who had almost destroyed him.

He rapped his knuckles against the door, managing to not rattle the whole thing. He stood and counted the seconds before he knocked again, but it opened first.

"Rachel?"

"No, hang on."

The blonde who'd answered disappeared, leaving Gordy standing in the doorway. He heard voices that were too low for him to understand. But then she reappeared.

"She's coming."

Before the girl walked away, Gordy heard a crisp order from somewhere inside the apartment. "For God's sake, don't leave him standing in the hallway."

The blonde glared at someone out of Gordy's line of sight. "He's not my friend. You let him in."

The door flew open. The woman locked him in a steady gaze as she gathered her head of curls and captured it in a thick hair tie. She dropped her hands to her hips.

"You're Gordy."

There was no note of question in her voice, only a

statement. The anger welled up inside him. "You must be Rachel."

She rubbed her fingers across her forehead and seemed to take a moment to collect her thoughts. "Sorry. You don't deserve my crappy attitude, but Sam hasn't been doing very well and seeing you at the door brought back everything that's keeping me up at night."

"His parents haven't talked to him in a few weeks. When they've called, he doesn't call them back."

"Shit, that's not good."

"They called me, so they must be worried."

She rubbed her hands over her face and sighed. A moment later she seemed to decide. "I can't remember when I talked to him last. I've tried to pull him out of the funk he's in, but nothing seems to matter." Guilt spread across her face. "I had tests today and haven't checked on him for a few days."

She ran to her room and grabbed a jacket. "I'll go with you. I bet we can find him if we work together." They took off down the hallway to begin their search.

* * * *

Gordy let the pickup roll to a stop in front of the building. His mood had changed. He was just worried about Sam at this point, regardless of their history. When he glanced at Rachel in the passenger seat, she seemed as worried as he felt.

"We looked everywhere. All of his friends. Any place he went to. Anyone. I..." Rachel lifted her hands and let them drop in a gesture of futility. There was a long silence then she continued. "You don't think he would have...?"

Gordy shook his head, even though he'd been thinking the same thing. "No. Sam would never hurt himself. He's a survivor. No doubt about it," Gordy said with a conviction he didn't have.

Rachel nodded and opened her door. Before she got out,

she twisted back to Gordy. "You'll give me a call, right? If you find out anything..."

"Don't worry. If I find him or hear anything, I'll let you know."

She nodded, jumped from the truck and disappeared inside without a backward glance.

Gordy was on autopilot as he drove toward his trailer. He'd been going step by step through the places they'd been during their time together. He thought he was missing something. It gnawed at him like a coyote on a fresh kill. He turned the corner, fishtailing down the road. With a thump, the biology textbook wedged against the windshield fell onto the seat beside him. Gordy stared at it for a second and realized the one place they hadn't checked.

He wrenched the steering wheel to the left and threw the big truck into as short of a U-turn as possible. He retraced his steps, ignoring any traffic laws. Slowing somewhat, he threaded his way through the maze of roads winding through campus. He got lucky and found a parking spot close to the library.

Gordy shot past people walking at a normal speed as he almost ran across the wide sidewalks coming to the triple doorway. He shot through the entrance and to the elevator. He hit the button a few times and glanced at the deep red LED numbers. *Third floor. Fuck!*

He glanced around, spotted the stairs and made a dash for them. The higher he climbed, the more urgent it became. He burst through the door to the fifth floor and stood gasping. Those closest to the stairs gave him an evil look, Gordy refused to let himself be affected.

He made his way through the stacks until he came to the wide wooden desk Sam had been sitting at on their first meeting. He turned the corner, knowing he was right.

Empty.

He dropped his hands to the tabletop to keep him from collapsing to the floor as hopelessness overwhelmed him. He'd just known Sam would be here. He was shocked he'd been wrong.

"Gordy?"

His head snapped up to find a thin, scruffy face and a sweatshirt that had to be several times too large curled into one of the tiny single-chair alcoves on this floor. It took a few seconds for him to recognize his former boyfriend.

"Sam? Is that you?" The sight in front of Gordy was shocking. The usually impeccably dressed Sam looked like a typical college stoner on a severe downward spiral. Gordy wasn't sure what he would feel when he found Sam, but after the hours of searching, he was happy to have found him. And he was alive.

Sam's expression went from jubilant to hardened in a few seconds. "Yeah, it's me. I'm fine. I need to study now. I have to pass the fucking classes to graduate."

"You don't look so good, man. Where have you been staying?"

Sam ran his hand over his face and seemed to realize his appearance. "Yeah, I guess. I haven't felt up to the whole gay grooming regime. And there's always some place to crash on campus, especially if you don't care too much." He gave Gordy a smile that never got to his eyes.

Gordy moved closer and Sam held out a shaking hand to stop him. "Really. I'm fine. I got into the whole getting-ready-for-finals thing."

Gordy stopped, trying to decide what he should do. "Your parents are worried about you. They called me to see if I'd seen you. Rachel's worried, too. We spent the night looking for you."

A tear ran along the side of Sam's nose that he scrubbed away with the oversized sleeve of the sweatshirt. "Okay. Thanks. I'll take care of it and make sure they don't bother you anymore."

Gordy stepped a little closer, and Sam recoiled. "Honest. It's fine. I'm sure I'm the last person on the planet you want to see. I get that." Sam shivered, and he wrapped his arms around himself. "I was as big a jerk as possible the last time we talked."

Gordy considered Sam. "Yeah, you were." Gordy took a deep breath, held it for a second before letting it out with a whoosh. "You were right, though. It's not fair that I'm not as out as you are."

Now, the tears were a steady stream down Sam's face but he said nothing else. Gordy took another step closer and noticed the sweatshirt. "My sweatshirt? I thought you'd burn all my stuff."

A sound like broken glass came from Sam. "I found it stuffed into the bottom of my bag the other day." His voice dropped to a hoarse whisper. "It smelled like you, and I missed that." He stared at Gordy for a minute and slumped into the chair. "I missed you. I love you."

The final emotional wall came crashing down. Those words didn't cure everything, but they could work on the problems. Gordy moved until he'd wedged himself into the chair with Sam, put an arm around his back and leaned in close. "I've missed you, too. I want our relationship."

Sam leaned into Gordy and he sensed the shiver going through his body. After a few seconds, Sam wiped his face with his sleeve. "I don't have much to offer. I may never be able to do everything you'd want."

Gordy kissed him on his cheek. "Have I ever complained? We can do whatever you'd like. I don't want us to have another meltdown. And you're right. I need to work more on being out."

Sam shook his head as he took Gordy's arm in his hands and gripped him tight. "That was so far out of line that I didn't think you could forgive me. You can't be out to everyone. I get that. You don't have the best safety net, and I attacked you about it."

Gordy shrugged but pushed himself out of the chair with a grunt of effort. He turned to Sam and extended his hand. "Come on. Let's get you cleaned up."

Sam smiled a little as he took the offered hand and unwound from the chair. "Is the funk that bad?"

He waited while Sam gathered his stuff and crammed them into his book bag. When Sam stood, his expression said he was expecting an answer. Instead, Gordy held out his phone. "Call your mother first, then Rachel. I promised both of them I'd call when I found you. I don't want either of those women mad at me." He paused for a moment before continuing, "And, yes, you're that funky. You have to shower before you get back in bed with me. I like your normal smell, but this is beyond sexy and appealing."

"We're going to your trailer?" There was a little catch in Sam's voice when he asked.

"Yeah, if you're okay with it." He smirked at Sam. "Obviously, you don't understand how to take care of yourself."

Sam smiled then stared at the screen on the phone. "I'll text Rachel. She can't blast me as far if it's through a text message."

Gordy glanced at Sam but kept his comments to himself as he pressed the elevator button.

Chapter Fifteen

The early morning sunshine lit the bedroom as Gordy drifted awake. Sam was snuggling tightly against him. Just the thought of Sam's scantily covered body curled along his caused Gordy to chub. While he wouldn't refuse something more intimate, he was satisfied for now. He'd been chewing on the issue he'd promised Sam he'd work toward. Coming out. He needed to do it. He knew it would be so much better to stop keeping his secret—his huge, life-altering, family-shattering, world-changing secret.

"What are you squirming around about so early on a Sunday morning?" Sam asked as he wriggled even tighter against Gordy. When he took Gordy's hand and pulled his arm over his chest, Gordy couldn't help but chuckle. "What's this? Am I your electric blanket?"

"No electricity needed. One hundred percent organically powered."

Gordy leaned in and kissed the back of Sam's neck. "I hate to ask when things are going so well for us, but how did yesterday's counseling session go?"

Sam snorted a little and pressed back against Gordy. "Fine, I guess. Same thing she always says. It wasn't my fault. Guys can be raped, too, and being gay had nothing to do with it." Sam sighed even louder. "It will take time, and there's no magic number of days. It's different for everyone. Same thing she's been saying since I started seeing her as a freshman."

"All of which makes perfect sense. Baby steps, little baby steps. We want you to get better."

"You're going to get tired of waiting."

"Oh, that's bullshit. It's not like we don't do anything. It'll be fine."

Sam slumped against the bed. "A few hand jobs and oral once. That's not going to keep a man at home."

"I have no intention of going anywhere else for sex. Relax and trust me. Now, we need to talk."

"Nothing good follows 'we need to talk'. What's up?"

"I've been thinking about what you said—about needing to come out."

Sam sat up on the bed and grabbed Gordy's hand. "Babe, I was mad at myself and a complete ass. You shouldn't take anything I said to heart. Please ignore that whole tirade."

Gordy shrugged and grinned. "It wasn't our best moment, but you were right. I need to live my life." He shrugged and a sad sigh escaped. "I can't chance my scholarships, so I still need to be careful around the other players."

"Does anyone on the team know?"

"Nate. But he's known for years."

"No one else?"

Gordy considered for a moment then shook his head. "Everyone else is a jerk—or too afraid of Coach Miller for me to trust. He's made it clear he doesn't want any of 'those people' on his team."

"Do you think your family would tell the coaches?"

"No, no way. However they react, they won't want anyone else to know."

"Okay, you have a plan, though." Sam sat for a moment. "They aren't going to hurt you, are they?"

Gordy started to answer, then closed his mouth. He stared into space for a minute before turning back. "My mother's going to unhinge. She's extremely religious, and gay is a big sin to her. The rest of them I'm not sure about. Dad doesn't agree with a lot of what Mom says, but it's not like there are many same-sex couples living in the backwoods of Oklahoma."

Sam kept his silence as he ran his fingers over Gordy's chest. Gordy was enjoying the intimate moment but hadn't finished with the discussion they were having. "Sam…"

He slowed his hand and shifted his gaze until their eyes met. "Yeah?"

"Would you go with me? To tell my family?"

Sam inhaled, held it for a few seconds then let the air bleed off. "You think that's a good idea? After showing up with your boyfriend, it changes the whole conversation. They'll say I've seduced you."

"Maybe not. I can be stubborn. But I'd like moral support. It would be nice if someone was on my side."

Sam considered Gordy for quite a while. A weight lifted when Sam nodded. "I will on one condition. We get a hotel room. I'm not staying at your parent's house. They need time to get used to the idea, and we'll want a place to recover." Their eyes locked. "But, yeah, I'll be your wingman."

Gordy chuckled. "I don't think you quite have the term wingman nailed down, but thanks for agreeing to come for moral support." He pulled Sam to his side and kissed his neck. Since they had gotten back together, Gordy had been careful to not press intimacy with Sam. They had been sleeping together, and it had been several days since he'd awoken to find Sam asleep on the built-in because he was feeling too confined. The help he was getting through the university did seem to be assisting his recovery, even if he hated to admit it.

Sam pressed closer until their torsos were tight against each other. He draped his arm around Sam, who nestled his head against Gordy's shoulder. He enjoyed the intimacy and was willing to give Sam all the time he needed. Gordy was contentedly scratching Sam's back when he started to speak.

"So, any more favors?" Sam asked.

"Nope. How about you?"

The silence drew out, but Sam had heard him.

"Gordy?"

"Yeah, Sam."

"I'm pretty horny this morning…"

A grin stretched across Gordy's face but he wanted Sam to make the moves. "Oh? And did you have something in mind to fix that problem?"

"I thought we might…like…try a little fun?"

"That sounds good. You lead the way and I'll follow. Anything you want to try works for me. If we do something and it doesn't feel right, we'll stop. No big deal. And if it gets too intense, we can stop the whole thing. We're just having fun. Okay?"

"You sure? Because I can't…"

Gordy leaned back in and kissed Sam's ear. "It will be good. So long as I'm with you, everything is fine."

Sam's hand shook as he trailed it across Gordy's chest. Gordy flipped the sheet off them and enjoyed the warmth of the eastern sun pouring through the window above. Where it hit the hair on Sam's thighs, there was a golden aura. Gordy reached lower, cupped his hand on the back of Sam's knee and drew his leg on top. His tight thigh and wonderful texture seeped into Gordy. Sam darting his hands across his chest sent another delicious layer of pleasure over him.

As the sensations built, Sam bent lower, flicked the tip of his tongue against Gordy's nipple and scraped it with his teeth. His response was immediate as blood pumped into his shaft. He cupped Sam's ass cheeks and squeezed them. The mutual sensations had him throbbing when Sam slid his hand lower to toy with the thick, dark trail running from his navel.

He surrendered to the sensations and rolled to his back with a sigh. "That's good. Really good."

Sam lifted his head, his face flushed and he was panting. "How about this?"

With a final tug at his treasure trail, Sam spread his hand over Gordy's crotch and rubbed his palm up and down the length of hard cock trapped in Gordy's compression shorts. He bucked a few times, wanting more of what Sam was dishing out. Gordy released himself to the pleasure.

He reached out and gripped Sam's hand, stopping him. Sam's face twisted in sudden panic, which Gordy dismissed with a chuckle and a wave. "Nothing's wrong. Actually, it was too good. I was about to lose it." He ran his fingertips along Sam's jaw. "I'd like to turn the tables on you."

By way of reply, Sam rolled to his back, closed his eyes and opened his legs. Gordy leaned in and kissed his chin, enjoying the tickle of copper whiskers against his lips. A soft sigh filled the air as he kissed his way down the center of Sam's throat. As he reached the dip at the base, he flicked his tongue out and ran the flat of it across the pale skin. The flavor of salty musk washed through his mouth.

Sam groaned and his head relaxed, opening his neck to Gordy. He ran his kisses higher until he found a tender spot below Sam's ear piercing. He licked, bit and sucked until Sam realized what he was doing and jerked away. His eyes shot open and he gave Gordy an accusatory look. "You'll give me a hickey."

Gordy turned his head with two fingers and smiled. "Too late. You've got a hickey."

"Gordy! What am I going to tell people?"

"That you turned your boyfriend on so much that he couldn't help himself."

Sam grinned and relaxed back against the bed. "So hot that you lost control, huh?"

"Yep, too hot." Before Sam could register another objection, he slipped his thumbs over Sam's small pink nipples and rubbed across them. Whatever Sam was about to say was lost in a groan that resonated through Gordy's body. He pressed his lips against first one nipple then the other until both of them were little more than hard red nubs of flesh. He pressed his lips down Sam's flat torso and teased lower. He moved to the side, tracing his fingers through the bright red hair trailing from Sam's navel. After a few more tugs from Gordy, Sam's hard cock was jerking inside his confining briefs.

"You're a cock tease."

"Oh? You think so?" Gordy said.

"Cock. Tease."

Gordy grinned, crawled between Sam's legs and gripped his package. "Still think I'm a tease?"

Sam's cock flexed like a freshly caught fish, and he was breathing in gasps. Gordy waited far longer than he wanted to in order to give Sam time to stop what they were doing. But he seemed much more interested in the sensations flowing through his body than any fears.

Gordy tugged the briefs down, a fraction of an inch at a time, until Sam's hard shaft was trapped in the final bit of cloth. Sam's expression was one of hunger as his chest heaved. Gordy tightened his grip and tugged off Sam's briefs. The hard column of flesh swung upward, trailing a translucent strand until it hit Sam's stomach with a wet smack.

Gordy crawled slowly each deliberate movement taking him closer to his goal. He paused when he could move no farther and Sam spread his legs.

"You ready to find out why we wanted to get all the damn testing done so we don't need rubbers?"

Sam nodded, and his cock twitched. Gordy eased closer until he pressed his nose into Sam's ball sac. He inhaled and held his breath to enjoy the scent before releasing it. He darted his tongue out and licked the base of Sam's cock. From there, he moved higher, coating the underside of the long shaft with spit. He slipped Sam's foreskin upward until it covered the knob then nipped at it, tugging it with his teeth.

Sam quivered under the attention. "Gordy." He gasped out. "I'm about to lose it."

Gordy leaned down, stuck his tongue in Sam's ample foreskin and flicked along the edge of the crown. Sam made a low growl and tensed as Gordy stroked him from tip to base in a slow release.

"Fuck! Do it. Stop teasing me."

Gordy chuckled but kept up his pace. Sam lasted for

several minutes before his muscles locked and, with a guttural groan, the first thick strand of white landed across his stomach. The next jet hit with a splat on his face and was quickly followed by the third strand. From that point onward, Gordy felt as if he was holding a water hose. By the time the last of the cum dribbled from Sam's dick, he'd sprayed himself from crotch to forehead. His breath came in gasps as Gordy leaned back to enjoy the scene of pleasure he'd created. He leaned across Sam's chest and ran his tongue through a large strand before leaning forward and kissing Sam.

"How was that?"

"Fuck. Holy fuck. My mind is blown." He licked his lips and grinned at Gordy. "Nice to find out my straight-laced boyfriend is a little kinky."

Heat flashed through Gordy's face, but before he could come up with a reply, Sam was crawling out of the bed. Filled with a moment of panic, Gordy fought with the urge to grab his arm. Before he could make a misstep, Sam turned back to him.

"Nothing's wrong. But before I start on you, I'm getting some of this stuff off me."

Gordy relaxed as Sam disappeared. A few seconds later, he heard water running and someone humming. *Sam? Humming? I have an after-sex hummer. Interesting.* Sam reappeared and tossed a wet washcloth onto the glass-topped nightstand. He crawled across the bed and lowered himself on top of Gordy.

Gordy cut his eyes to the washcloth. "Planning ahead?"

"Hell, yes. I plan on having you so horned up that you'll coat both of us."

Gordy relaxed, letting the worry that Sam might have an episode slip away as he enjoyed the sensations of having Sam on top of him. A tingle flashed through his system as Sam rolled his nipples between his fingers. A few heartbeats later, he realized he was stiff again, and this time, someone else noticed. It would have been difficult to miss, since Sam had wiggled until he was using Gordy as a mattress. Their crotches ground against each other, even if Sam's monster was drained for the moment.

A bite on his pec brought Gordy back to the present, the sharp pain washing over him in an erotic pulse. He realized what Sam had done to him.

"Hey! Now everyone'll see the hickey when we shower."

"Tell them your boyfriend was marking his territory and to be glad I didn't feel the need to piss on you to do it."

"Gross," Gordy said.

The next sensations to rip through him left Gordy the one panting when his nipples were released.

"Sensitive nips, good to know. Now, are you going to behave?"

Gordy smirked. "You going all alpha on me now?"

Sam smiled in a way that endeared him even more. "Maybe, a little. I kind of like bossing the giant football player around."

Gordy dropped back to the bed and winked at Sam. "Have fun."

He slipped between Gordy's legs and had his compression shorts off and flying across the room in a matter of seconds. Then he opened one of the nightstand drawers and pulled out a bottle of lube. He put a few squirts on Gordy's cock before wrapping his fingers around its thickness and squeezing. The tight, slick combination drove Gordy closer to a climax with each stroke. They'd been playing too long. He knew he wouldn't last.

A second later, the hand vanished and Gordy groaned at Sam. "Why'd you stop? I was so close."

"This is why."

Sam coated two fingers with lube and pressed them between Gordy's ass cheeks. He gasped at the delicious sensation, but before he could catalog it, Sam found his target and slithered two long, wet fingers into Gordy. As Sam clipped his sweet spot, Gordy knew the edging had ended.

His muscles locked, and he thrust upward as the first stream of cum spewed across both of them. In a rolling series of convulsions, Gordy released blast after blast of white lava over the two of them. Sam knelt between Gordy's widespread legs, hitting his prostate with every inward shove. A deep, rolling growl signaled the final wave of Gordy's orgasm.

Sam let his fingers slip out and cleaned the two of them with the damp cloth. The sensation left Gordy feeling very contented, even with the slight burning coming from his butt. Once Sam finished cleaning them both, Gordy motioned him back into bed and nestled his bare body against Sam as he held him. He kissed Sam on the cheek and whispered, "Are you okay?"

Sam chuckled as he wriggled closer to Gordy. "Never better. That was amazing. Everything was mind-blowing."

"And?"

Sam's expression was pure confusion for several seconds before he realized what Gordy was asking. "No. No nasties. No flashbacks. Just one fucking hot boyfriend who is great in bed."

Gordy grinned and pulled them even closer together to enjoy their moment of contentment.

Chapter Sixteen

They pulled into the driveway of a typical southeastern Oklahoma ranch. The house was white and sturdy with buildings, pens and equipment sprawling around it. The tractor alone was bigger than the trailer he and Sam had been sharing for the past several months. Familiar and comforting, the farm he grew up on had always been his support since he had been old enough to remember. The giant hay barn they filled every summer and emptied each winter served as a hideout without peer on rainy spring days. This might be his last visit to the family place for the rest of his life.

He glanced at Sam and got a small smile of support. Gordy took a deep breath and let it leak out. "I guess we should go in. It's not going to get any easier."

"Whatever you want to do, babe. I'm here for you."

He gave Sam a doubtful smile. "I appreciate you coming with me. It'll be about as much fun as pouring vinegar over a sunburn, but I'm glad to have someone backing me up."

Sam chuckled a little. "That sounds painful, so I'll take your word for it."

"It's getting hot in here. If we don't go inside, we'll need to drive around to cool off."

Sam lifted his hands and shrugged but made no comment.

"Fuck, let's do it. Come on." Gordy popped open the pickup door at the same time as Sam. The scorching air was like a blast furnace as they left the vehicle and started toward the fence. The sun-bleached concrete walk seemed longer than ever before. His gut knotted. He was gambling everything to live his own life.

Gordy reached the porch and raised his hand. He let a shaking fist slip to his side and turned to Sam. "I guess I don't need to knock."

"Probably not. Try to be calm."

His hand shook as he reached for the door. Gordy stopped and squeezed it into a tight fist. "I can do this."

He opened the door and cool dimness enveloped them. He moved through the living room, wondering where everyone was. Then he heard a low mumble and realized where they were. He turned back to Sam and whispered, "Kitchen."

He moved the last steps into what had been his favorite place growing up. Now he'd rather stick his arm in a branding fire than enter the room. He was trying to gather his courage when his little sister spotted him, ran across the room and wrapped her arms around him.

"Gordy! What are you doing? We're making sugar cookies. I picked them because they're your favorite. The first batch is about to come out of the oven." She glanced past him and smiled at Sam. "Gordy, who's your cute friend?"

"Heather Marie, we don't treat guests like that. I'm sure you've embarrassed Gordon's friend," his mother said.

Gordy gathered his courage to finish what he needed to do today. "Where's Jeff? I have something to tell everyone, and I don't want to do it but once."

Heather motioned to the back hallway. "He's in his bedroom. Hannah's here, too. She's taking a nap before Tyler wakes up."

Gordy cringed. The only person who could make this worse was his older sister, Hannah. "Get 'em. I want to get this over with."

Heather trotted a few feet down the hall and bellowed. "Jeff! Hannah! Get in here. Gordy wants to talk to everyone."

His brother stumbled into the kitchen, trying to tame his usual case of bedhead. The next thing Gordy heard was the staccato sound of his nephew's tiny feet racing down the hallway. The toddler spotted him and ran at him as fast as

143

he could. Gordy forgot his apprehension for a moment as he grabbed the youngster in his arms. His heart melted, and he had to hold his eyes shut when Tyler wrapped his arms around his neck and squeezed him tight. After a second or two, he released his favorite uncle and pointed behind them.

"Who's he?"

Gordy's head swam. He'd forgotten Sam. But before he could do anything. Sam stepped forward and grinned at Tyler. "I'm Sam. What's your name?"

"I'm Tyler. I'm Uncle Gordy's nose guard."

"That's way cool."

"Gordy, son. Tell us what's weighing on you. I can tell it's important for you," his dad said.

Gordy nodded and tried to gather his thoughts. But every set of words he'd put together for this moment had evaporated. He took in each member of his family, seeing varied levels of confusion and concern. When the time stretched to an uncomfortable length, Heather moved over and squeezed his arm.

"It'll be okay, big brother. Tell us."

Gordy scrubbed his face with his sleeve several times. He tried to get out the words. His vocabulary shrinking to something much less than Tyler's. Sam stepped closer as his family looked at each other. Suddenly words shot from Gordy's mouth and he had no control over them. "I'm gay and Sam's my boyfriend."

Jeff started laughing. "Well, it's about time. I just won a 'Get Out of Jail Free' card."

Heather stepped between the two of them and hugged them tightly. She studied Sam for a second before turning to Gordy and winking. "My brother has good taste."

Hannah's face contorted. Closing the distance between them, she grabbed Tyler from his arms and twisted away. Gordy thought his heart would break. He heard sobbing and turned to see his mother collapse onto one of the kitchen chairs. She kept muttering something that Gordy wasn't able to make out. As the crescendo climaxed, the oven timer buzzed, signaling the batch of cookies was finished.

"All right. Everyone calm down," Gordy's dad said. "Jeff, get the cookies. Jean, pull yourself together. It's not like the boy's dying. Let's go talk about this in the living room."

They moved into the darkened room, and Jeff flipped on a few lights as he flopped bonelessly onto one sofa while Gordy and Sam moved to the other. Their parents moved to the his and hers recliners while Hannah had an increasingly irate Tyler in her lap on the couch with Jeff.

His mother was devastated. She held a tea towel in her hand and was wiping her eyes as she crumbled into the chair as if her bones had turned to gelatin. Gordy took strength that his father was his normal unflappable self. Once the shuffling and adjusting stopped, his father studied him. Gordy felt uncomfortable with the silence when his father began.

"So, you think you're gay?"

"Yes, sir. Except, I don't think I'm gay. I *am* gay."

"How long have you known? Was it when you started college? Something you experimented with there?"

"No, sir. I've known I was attracted to other guys since before junior high."

His father appeared puzzled. "Why didn't you tell us before? You've kept this secret for all that time?"

"I didn't tell you because I was afraid you'd throw me out of the house or send me off to one of those places that claim they can cure people of being gay."

His mother straightened in the chair, her hands clenched. "The pastor preached about homosexuality last Sunday. He said there are places to get help."

Gordy's dad turned to her and shook his head. "Didn't you hear what the boy said? He's known since he was little and wouldn't tell us because he was afraid we'd do what you're suggesting. Besides, I might not be in church every time the doors open, but I consider myself a God-fearing man. Doesn't seem He screws up on these kind of things."

"But Doug—"

"Jean. I'm not throwing any of my kids away. Gordy's a bright man. If he says it's not a choice, I believe him." His attention shifted to Sam.

"Young man, are you my son's friend?"

Gordy rested his hand on Sam's shoulder. After a quick glance, Sam cleared his throat and nodded. "Yes, I'm Gordy's friend."

"You came with him for moral support?"

"Yes, sir. Gordy asked me to come, and I said I would."

Doug nodded and studied the two of them for a minute. "And you two are dating?"

This time, nervousness shook Sam. Gordy started to let Sam take the heat for him, but he refused to do that.

"Dad, we're dating—Sam and I."

Doug eased backward and steepled his fingers. Gordy noticed his mother seemed to have gotten herself together, at least for the moment. Once his dad's questions ended, it seemed safe to look at his brother and sisters.

Jeff was smiling and shaking his head. *He wasn't kidding. All the crap he's pulled and now he gets a pass. I'm the black sheep of the family—or at least that's what he's hoping.* But he'd never worried about how his brother would handle the news, so long as it didn't interfere with his partying or getting laid by whatever easy girl he dated that month. His brother definitely thought more with his little head than the big one. But the grin on his face said he was enjoying his older brother having crashed and burned for now.

Heather bumped against his leg, her grin stretching from ear to ear. He waited then glanced at Sam, who appeared ready to puke. When he glanced back at Heather though, she mouthed 'he's cute' to Gordy. At that point, Gordy couldn't help himself. He smiled from ear to ear.

That is, until he glimpsed his older sister. Her glare showed that she judged him harshly. Even worse, she held Tyler as if she were protecting him from a virulent plague. Some of his extended family would judge him based on things out of his control, but he'd never imagined Hannah would keep Tyler from him. He loved his nephew, and it would kill him if he couldn't see Tyler again. Tears gathered at the corner of his eyes when he considered it. But there was nothing he could do, and Gordy refused to tear up at this point.

His parents... His mother sat, sobbing and dabbing her eyes with a towel, but he'd expected her reaction. Her church was so rigid that it still didn't believe in interracial couples. Any church that wouldn't welcome Nate and Sarah was sad already. But based on her church, it would have been better if he'd been a murderer. Taking a life was more forgivable for them than loving someone of the same sex. It was the church that left Gordy scared and depressed through most of his junior high and high school days. Sports had been his outlet for the emotions. He'd earned a reputation in their district as a rough tackle. But he'd been fighting for his life.

Gordy's dad leaned forward, and the room dropped to silence. He studied Gordy for a minute before glancing at Sam. "I need a little time to consider all this, but you're my son and I'll always love you."

"Daddy! How can you condone this? It's not natural," Gordy's older sister blurted out.

"Hannah Michelle, you can't talk about anyone." He flicked his eyes at Tyler. "And so far as natural, Gordy says it's natural for him. He's never lied to me before. I don't see any reason to not trust him."

She started to say something else, but Doug cut her off with a motion of his hand. "Not another word. My children are always safe in my house. I don't believe Gordy's feelings are unnatural. A religion condemning someone because of who they love is what's unnatural."

He turned to his wife. "Jean, why don't you go to the bedroom and clean up? Your makeup's smeared. Everything will be fine. We want Gordy to be happy, whoever it's with. Right, dear?"

She wiped her eyes again and stood. She walked over and gave Gordy a kiss on the cheek and a smile to Sam. It was more than Gordy had expected, and he appreciated her effort. He stood and motioned to Sam before he gave his family a tight smile.

"We rented a hotel room in Ardmore. I thought it would be easier. Sam and I can stay there. We've already checked in and left our bags. I've dropped enough bombshells for one day. What if we grab something to eat in town and we'll be out tomorrow for lunch after church?"

His father studied him then nodded. "You're welcome here anytime, son, and Sam, too. But you're right. It might be better to let the emotions settle and everyone relax." He stood, wrapped his arms around Gordy and gave him a hug that ended with a back thumping series of pats. He offered a handshake to Sam, but after a second or two, he bear-hugged Sam, too. When he released Sam, he was beaming.

"Go to the hotel. Get something for supper and unwind. We'll see you tomorrow."

Gordy nodded, shot a smile around the room and exited, herding Sam ahead of him.

* * * *

Sam sat quietly, still shaken by the experience with Gordy's family. It could have gone much worse, but he hoped Gordy's dad stayed as supportive. The town wasn't striking, although he could make out the silhouette of the Arbuckle Mountains to their north. Gordy had been quiet since they'd left, and Sam planned to give him the space and time to consider the huge step he'd made.

The sun moved into the western horizon, the heat no longer rippled off the asphalt in waves and the breeze coming through open windows helped a little at cooling them off. He realized they were traveling away from the interstate and into a new part of town. When he glanced again at Gordy, his expression said he was a million miles away.

"Hey, Earth to Gordy. What's up?"

Gordy jumped in his seat and glanced at Sam. A moment later he smiled. "It went better than I was afraid it would. I wasn't sure about Dad. He was the big unknown."

Sam nodded. "Yeah, he seemed okay with everything. Hell, he even hugged me, and it didn't become some kind of python death hug."

Gordy shook his head and chuckled. "No, no python grip."

"Your sister…"

He shrugged. "I knew she wouldn't get it. I didn't think about her keeping Tyler away from me. I hope she doesn't stick with that attitude."

Sam nodded, but there was nothing he could add to the discussion. After another turn or two, he was certain they weren't driving toward the hotel any longer. He glanced at Gordy but he had again dropped into his own world.

"Hey, isn't the hotel the other direction?"

When he glanced over, Sam was glad to see the typical happy expression back on Gordy's face.

"We should get something to eat. There's a local place down here you'll like. It's called Burgers and Fries. Best hamburgers in town."

At the mention of food, Sam's stomach growled, not a surprising response considering neither of them had been hungry all day. It had been the stress playing with them, but now they were starving.

"They better be well stocked. I've seen you eat when you're hungry."

Gordy laughed but didn't disagree. A minute later they were parking at a typical small-town takeout joint. The parking lot was huge for such a tiny place. Gordy found a shaded spot to the side to keep the pickup from turning into an oven while they ate then walked with Sam to the building perched on a corner of the lot. They stood in front of the menu as Sam tried to decide. He glanced at Gordy and found him staring with a big happy grin across his face.

"You must already know what you want, so tell me what's good."

"Maybe so. But everything's good. I'm getting the triple cheeseburger basket. The chili dogs are tasty, too."

Sam studied the board for a minute and smiled at Gordy, who was acting more like a nine-year-old in town for a treat. This place was more about memories than the food. He glanced again at the menu board and decided.

He followed Gordy to the window and listened as he told the girl what he wanted. Once he'd finished, he motioned to Sam. "We're together, so put his meal on the same ticket."

The girl turned to him. Sam leaned closer. "Yeah. Umm. How about a foot-long chili dog, fries and a shake?"

"What flavor?"

"Oh yeah. Vanilla, I guess."

Gordy leaned in close and whispered, "Vanilla, yeah. Right."

Sam swatted him like a pesky fly as the girl looked up. Gordy paid for their meal, and it seemed only a few minutes before bag after bag of food was passed through the window to them. Sam glanced around, not sure where they would eat. Gordy pointed toward the wooded area behind the diner. "They have tables along a little creek. Let's eat out there."

They rounded the building and found the place Gordy had described. It didn't take long for them to tear the bags open and devour their food. Sam didn't realize how hungry he was until he took his first bite. The next few minutes were spent shoving food into his mouth as fast as possible.

"Mind if I join you?"

Sam's head shot up like it was on a spring. He relaxed to see Gordy's younger brother.

"Hey, Jeff. What's up?" When he waved at an empty seat, Gordy nodded. "Sure. Take a load off."

Jeff draped himself over the attached bench. Sam couldn't help but notice how different the two brothers were from each other. When Jeff winked at him and ate off Gordy's food, it confirmed his impression. Gordy rolled his eyes and moved his meal out of reach. When Jeff reached for Sam's fries, he cocked an eyebrow and picked up one of the plastic knives. "Just so you understand the rules, I stab people who eat off my plate."

Gordy snorted but kept silent as Jeff shot him a charming smile but didn't try again. He turned back to Gordy as he crossed his arms and leaned against the seat. He gave Gordy a shit-eating grin that left Sam wanting to scrub it off his face.

"So, thanks about the whole gay thing. You took the heat off me for at least a little while until the parental units remember to watch me as close."

"As much as it pains me to tell you, I didn't come out to the family to distract them from your stunts."

Jeff dropped his gaze to the ground, and the quiet stretched out. When he looked back at them, Sam saw the family resemblance with no trouble. He'd changed to a serious expression when he met Gordy's gaze.

"I'm serious, man. What you did took a lot of balls."

Sam almost piped up with a crack about Gordy's balls but stopped himself just in time. This was a serious moment between the brothers, and he didn't need to disrupt it.

Gordy had been staring at his sibling but nodded. "That was the hardest thing I've ever done. I've heard too many stories about how coming out can go wrong. Some of them will never get over it, but I've done what I needed to. I can't tell everyone yet, but this is a big start."

Sam reached up, took Gordy's hand in his and gave it a squeeze. "You did good. Come out however works for you. Telling the world over Facebook isn't for everyone."

He slipped his hand off Gordy's and glanced over to see how Jeff dealt with their private moment. He found Jeff staring at the ground with his face having turned a bright crimson. Sam studied Jeff as he spoke.

"I don't know if I'll ever have the guts to tell them," Jeff said in a low voice.

Gordy scowled at his brother. "Don't try to tell me that you're gay. You have boinked any girl that will let you crawl between her legs."

Jeff nodded slowly. "There's a time when a guy wants fish, but sometimes nothing satisfies like beef."

"No way. You're fucking with me." An angry glower grew on Gordy's face, but Sam had noticed something about Jeff, and he waved Gordy down. "He's not bullshitting. Are you, Jeff?"

Gordy's brother shook his head and he met Gordy's gaze. "I've been looking online. I think I'm bisexual. It's kind of hard to tell. I seem to be attracted to all kinds of people."

Gordy still didn't seem appeased. "You're just milking this so I think you aren't the biggest pussy hound in Ardmore. You've never been with a guy, have you?"

Jeff looked as uncomfortable as Sam had seen him so far, and his answer almost disappeared in a gust of wind. "Yeah, I've been with a guy. It's different—but good."

"No way! You're lying. Who was it? If you aren't fucking, you're playing video games with Charlie." Gordy stared at his brother and blurted out. "Charlie? It's *Charlie*?"

Jeff glanced around and hissed. "Holy shit, would you keep it down?"

Gordy dropped his volume, but Sam could tell he was just starting his tirade. "You're a horny seventeen-year-old who'd make it with anything on two legs and now you're trying to find some excuse for your behavior."

Jeff flipped Gordy off with both hands and started to leave. "Fuck you, you sanctimonious prick. You want everyone to accept that you like guys, but you classify me as some kind of pervert because I don't fit in your category of gay. Well, fuck you and the horse you rode in on. Or does that mean I have sex with horses? You should tell me how it works, genius brother."

Gordy inhaled, his glare turning dark. Sam stood, a palm toward each of them. "Stop it. Just stop it. This is a fucking stupid argument, and it's stopping right now."

He focused on Gordy. "Your brother came out to you. You should be honored that he trusted you, not ripping him a new asshole."

Jeff started to speak but Sam cut him off, "You're no better. It's tough to label an identity. Some gay guys identify as bi at first and settle later to gay, but it's equally valid to be bi. You've gotta give people a little time to get use to the new information."

Sam waved his hand in the space separating the two. "But this? This bitching? It's stupid, and you're hurting your family. Stop it and talk."

They gave up their staring war at the same instant. "Do you have feelings for anyone?"

Jeff shrugged then sagged back into his seat. "Charlie and I have been buddies since forever. But his family... Well, he's afraid they'd kill him. He's sure they'd throw him out. We have to be careful. I'd do anything for him, but I don't know if we're more than friends with benefits. Girls are good, too, but it's different. It's not like being with a guy. Not just the equipment, either. It's... I don't know how to explain it." His gaze hardened for a moment. "And I haven't had sex with that many girls — only a couple. Charlie and I were together then, too. He kind of knew, but we never talked about what we were."

Gordy glanced first at Sam, who only arched an eyebrow. Then he turned to Jeff. "Sorry that I was being a huge ass. You feel however you do about other people, and I have no right to tell you otherwise."

Jeff shrugged. "We're better helping each other. Otherwise, it'll be a miserable life."

Gordy stood up and opened his arms. "Is a hug okay?"

Jeff rolled his eyes before grinning. "Of course."

He wrapped his arms around Gordy and squeezed. *It must run in the family because that hug looks a lot like the one Doug gave me.* Gordy let go and stepped away. He reached down and pushed what was left of his food toward Jeff.

"Want fries?"

* * * *

The road didn't seem as long and narrow as yesterday when they'd driven toward the Hager ranch. But today he wasn't afraid of the backlash of an angry family against their golden boy's lover. Gordy's mom would learn to live with it. She wouldn't brag about making a quilt for her son and his husband, but she would tolerate him to see her son.

The pickup hit a deep pothole and tossed Sam against the windshield, bringing his attention back to the present. They were traveling down an aged county road that hadn't had the blacktop repaired in several decades. Ridges of white stones peered through the tawny and green of early spring. With red cattle moving from one tuft of grass to another, tails lazily snapping away flies, it was an idyllic setting.

"When did your family move here?"

Gordy glanced at him and realized he actually wanted to know. "Late eighteen hundreds. They came up from Texas when the Indian Territory lands was sold off."

"Wow, almost a hundred and fifty years. I have no idea where my family was at that point in history. Maybe still in Ireland."

They rode quietly for several minutes before Sam spoke again. "Think any of my ancestors were gay" — he turned to grin at Gordy — "or bi?"

Gordy chuckled and playfully punch Sam on the shoulder, a little harder than Sam expected. *I'll leave that subject alone for a while.* He rubbed his shoulder but when he looked at Gordy, he was considering the question.

"Well, both sides of my family came from the south. There were all kinds of bachelor uncles and spinster aunts, so who knows? As for anyone who's bi? I have no idea. If anyone knew, it didn't make it into the general family history."

They bounced again as Gordy tried to dodge another set of holes, with more success. Sam sat back to relax and Gordy started again. "If I remember from my freshman history and sexuality class, the Celts didn't have a problem with same sex pairings, so you'd have been in good company, at least before Christianity came along."

"And when might that be, oh-source-of-all-knowledge?"

"Hmm, fifth century, I think—Saint Patrick and all that good stuff." Gordy sat for a few moments before shaking his head. "Hannah is like dealing with Morgana. She's determined to screw up everything."

Sam started to say something then dropped his gaze. He glanced up to find Gordy watching him. "What?"

Sam waved him off and shook his head. "One of those times when I need to keep my mouth shut. Don't worry about it."

With lips pressed into a short, thin line Gordy glared at Sam. "Just tell me. Please."

Sam considered being difficult, but another glance at Gordy confirmed his initial choice would be a poor one. "Okay. But remember you insisted. I told you it was stupid."

"Got it. Now, what?"

"It's Carman."

Gordy's face glazed over in confusion. "What's Carman? What the hell are you talking about?"

"Carman is the evil witch from Irish mythology. Morgana is the witch from the King Arthur stuff."

With a blank face, Gordy stared at Sam. The pickup hit the gravel shoulder and lurched sideways. After a few seconds of chaos, Gordy had the truck stopped, and his forehead was resting on the steering wheel. Sam reached closer to Gordy's shaking form, afraid he'd injured himself, but Gordy snorted and it echoed through the cab. He tilted his face toward Sam and let the tears of laughter roll down his cheek.

"You're correcting my mythology?"

"Yes," Sam agreed with hesitation.

Gordy twisted his head and tapped it against the wheel with his body still shaking with laughter. After a few more seconds, he gasped out, "Can we agree she is a witch, regardless of mythos?"

Sam's muscles unclenched as he relaxed. "I can go with that. But let's get back on the road. I'd like to be headed north before anything bad happens."

Gordy backed up, slammed the vehicle in first gear and dug his way out of the loose gravel. He raced through the other gears until they were again shooting down the road. The silence that enveloped them echoed their tension as they got closer to the ranch. By the time they turned into the entrance, their unease had grown by a huge factor. The truck rolled to a stop, but neither of them made a move to get out.

"It's about the same as yesterday, maybe even a little better. Right?"

Sam stared straight ahead but nodded. "Yeah. About the same."

Still, they sat, waiting. Sam realized two figures had left the house, and Gordy tensed. He studied the two for a few seconds then muttered. "That's Charlie with Jeff, isn't it?"

"Oh yeah, that would be Charlie."

Sam watched as the two walked toward them. Gordy rolled down his window when they were close. They studied the younger pair, and Jeff grinned. "Relax, big brother. I haven't caused any trouble. Just thought I'd let you know everything's cool."

"So Mom and Dad are okay?"

"Seem to be, yeah. Hannah still looks like she's been sucking limes, but it's been years since she was happy. Heather's probably sewing you a rainbow flag, but you knew she'd be on your side."

Gordy cocked his head a little and flicked it toward Charlie. Jeff narrowed his eyes, leaned closer and Sam struggled to hear him. "Don't. I wasn't kidding. His dad might kill him. Charlie's terrified that they'll find out."

"Why is he with you?"

"We've been friends since forever. It just happened. But I

swore I wouldn't tell anyone, so you can't, either."

Sam studied the other young man. He was tall and slender, his light blond hair in one of the latest styles, but something was wrong in his stance. Not only did he keep his arms folded across his chest, but he stood with anything other than confidence. His pressed white long-sleeved shirt looked as crisp as he looked defeated and desolate. Sam kept an eye on him while Gordy and Jeff talked in whispers. Whatever he was dealing with, it wasn't good.

"Ready to go inside? It's getting hot out here."

Sam glanced away from Charlie, who was a huge puzzle to Sam. "Sounds good. Let's see how things go."

Sam popped open his door and followed Gordy and Jeff into the house. He stopped at the open doorway and turned back to Charlie, who paced across the narrow sidewalk. Sam worried about the boy, but they'd met all of five minutes ago, and he had no reason to trust Sam with anything serious. But Sam couldn't help himself, he felt like he had to say something.

"Charlie. You coming in?"

He stopped in mid-stride and his gaze fixed on Sam. He stood there for a minute before taking a single trembling step toward the house. Once he was close to Sam, he whispered. "You're Gordy's boyfriend?"

"Yeah."

"And people don't hate you?"

The question startled Sam, and he considered giving an easy answer. But he stopped himself. Charlie deserved a more complete response.

"Most people don't care. Some are supportive. But some people? Well, some people hate me, but I don't understand why."

"My daddy says gay people are going to hell."

Sam felt a too-familiar twist in his gut. "Being gay is not going to send anyone to hell. I don't think God messes up when he makes people."

Charlie moved at an even more frantic pace until Sam

thought he'd shoot apart like an old-fashion clock. But his shoulder sagged, and he stood staring at the ground. Sam let Charlie calm himself before stepping closer. He let his hand hover then realized such familiarity might not be welcome. He let his hand drop but stayed beside Charlie.

"Let's go inside. It's just the Hagers. You've been over here tons of times."

Charlie nodded and followed behind Sam as they entered the dim interior of the house. All Sam heard was the quiet hum of the air conditioning and a conversation going on in the next room he couldn't quite make out. He stood next to Charlie and wondered where everyone had gone. The whole Hager clan flooded the room at once. Gordy's dad flipped on the television to catch the game with his favorite state team.

"Dad, you're being a traitor again. You're supporting the enemy. Traitor! You're kill'n me!" Gordy said.

His dad frowned and motioned him into silence. "This isn't like a real game. I recorded it and already know who wins. Besides, I always cheer for State when you play them."

Gordy shook his head as if it were the end of the world, but Sam saw from his almost-invisible smile this was a familiar taunt between the two of them. Gordy's mother went back into the kitchen and Hannah and Heather soon joined her while the guys watched the game. The first quarter was close to ending when Jean came to the door, drying her hands on a tea towel.

"Turn that noise off and wash up. We're putting dinner on the table."

Doug hovered for a minute before clicking the remote and plunging the room into darkness. Without a word, they filed to the bathroom to wash up for dinner. Gordy and Jeff led the way, horsing around as usual. Their father cleared his throat and the two truants calmed down. It got to his turn, and he motioned Charlie ahead of him. "Go ahead. I need a minute or two alone in the bathroom before I wash up."

Charlie nodded and stepped in front of Sam. At first, he was staring vacantly into space but then the sight before him registered. There were spots of pink across the white shirt on Charlie's back. Horror filled Sam when he realized some of them seemed to be stuck.

"Charlie, what's wrong with your back?"

His jaw clenched, and he yanked part of his shirt free with a guttural noise. "I better get home. I gotta go."

Sam didn't even try to argue. "Gordy. Come here please, like right now!"

There was a scrape of chair legs against wooden floor then boots coming closer. He glanced toward Charlie and saw he was trying to back toward the door. "Don't, Charlie. Please."

Gordy walked beside them at that moment and shot them both a confused look. "What's up? Mom has lunch ready, and she hates it when stuff gets cold."

Sam nodded at the ghost pale man in front of them. "Check out his back."

Gordy's brow furrowed, and he glanced between the two of them. His expression became grave as he focused his attention. "What's going on, Charlie?"

"Nothing. Honest, Gordy. I just got in trouble this morning."

His scowl deepened. "Let me see."

Charlie appeared close to bursting into tears as he turned so his back was facing them. There was a moment of silence and when Sam glanced at Gordy, his jaw clinched at the sight before him.

"What are you kids doing? Your mother has lunch ready."

"Dad, we need you for a minute."

There was only silence before Doug appeared at his side. He was grim when Gordy nodded toward Charlie. After a few seconds, he reached over, pinched the shirt's cloth, then with the lightest of touches pulled the material away from Charlie's back. A whimper leaked out that made Sam wince.

"How bad is it?" Doug asked. The dark expression on his face was more ominous than any hell-bringer thunderstorm.

Charlie made a tiny motion of denial. "I didn't get chores done fast enough and messed up the tractor."

"Your dad did this?"

Charlie answered, although it was obvious to Sam that he wasn't asking a question. "Yes, sir. But I screwed up. I know better."

Jeff rounded the corner as Charlie finished what he was saying, spotted the blood dotted shirt and turned a deep shade of red. Without a word, he lifted the shirt a little and exposed a pattern of bruises and bleeding marks.

"I'm killing the fucker! He can't keep doing this to you." He charged toward the door, but Gordy grabbed his arm.

"Charlie's hurt, and charging off half-cocked won't help anyone."

"Get your damn hands off me," Jeff snarled.

Doug leveled a gaze at the two of them that would have frozen fire. "That's enough."

The battling brothers stopped, seeming chastised. Doug's focus shifted back to the young man who was standing a few feet from him and trembling. "Charlie. I need you to take off your shirt, so I can see how bad the injuries are."

He shook like a cottonwood leaf during a summer storm. Sam was almost certain Charlie had tears running down his face. "Mr. Hager, please. I'll go home. I didn't know they were still bleeding."

A firm voice cut through the air. "Everyone go sit down and leave us alone."

It was Gordy's mother. This wasn't the woman who had been so overwhelmed at Gordy's news that she needed help to move. This clearly was a woman Sam didn't want to fuck with, and God help him or anyone else who messed with her kids. It was obvious she considered Charlie a child of hers.

But she underestimated her family. Not only did no one leave, but Heather and Hannah were listening. She snorted a divisive comment, but turned back to Charlie. "Apparently, no one will listen. Let's get you out of this dark hallway and see how bad it is." She fixed a still-furious Jeff with an unflinching stare. "Get me a bucket of hot water and a washcloth."

"For what?" Jeff snarled.

She studied him for a minute but answered his question, "To soak the shirt loose. Some places it's dried and I don't want to tear anything open."

At this point, an overwhelmed Charlie moved into the well-lit dining room. A minute into the process, Jean asked the girls to take Tyler outside to play. Halfway through, it was obvious Charlie was in pain getting his shirt off his slender body. Jeff stepped to his side and took his hand. A glance passed between Doug and Jean but neither spoke.

The tension was palpable by the time Charlie could slip his shirt from his back. Sam was horrified and gasped, but the expressions on the faces of the four members of Gordy's family were terrifying. If Gordy on the football field was anything close to as fearsome, the opposing tackles would run the other direction.

Jean darted her hand and hovered over Charlie's back like a hummingbird but never made contact. After a few seconds, she took a deep breath and shook her head. "We need to take you to the hospital, Charlie."

That panicked the young man and tears flowed again. "No, please. I can't go to the hospital. I can't. I'll go home. They'll close up soon. I just forgot to wear a T-shirt under my shirt."

Sam was dumbstruck by the sight in front of him, and what Charlie was telling them had happened before. Seven or eight purple and blue welts covered his back with the bloody marks seeping from far too many places. He saw why Jean was hesitant to begin. Jeff was pale and holding tightly to Charlie's hand. It occurred to Sam that he could help. He didn't have the years of history with Charlie to make this as emotion-laden. He slipped closer and took the opened first-aid box from Jean's hand and guided Charlie to a seat.

Sam ignored everyone as he slipped on a pair of gloves from the kit. He studied the crisscrossing wounds and tried to remember the Red Cross first-aid training he'd had years before. Sam grabbed two of largest pads in the kit and soaked the first one with peroxide. He patted the most severe places along Charlie's shoulders. The initial couple of times he touched the lacerated areas got a hissing inhalation. But as he moved lower, leaving a trail of foaming peroxide and clean skin, the reaction lessened. Before he'd gotten more than a short way down the young man's back, Gordy had stepped in, donned another pair of gloves stretched to their limit by his massive hands and applied antibiotic ointment with obvious care.

Time lost all relevance as he worked his way down the pale back in front of him. He reached the end of the expanse of skin and studied the sullen red marks disappearing into his pants. He glanced at Gordy and got a slight shake of his head. Sam picked up a roll of gauze and paused for a moment before turning to Gordy.

"I don't know if this will make it worse. Is it going to stick again?"

Gordy studied Charlie for an instant then turned back to Sam. "He can wear one of my old T-shirts. It'll be so big on him that it won't touch anything." He disappeared down the hallway and reappeared a minute later with an oversized dark orange T-shirt in his hands. He held it out to Charlie, who slipped it over his torso. The shirt seemed to relieve the anxious young man.

Jean and Gordy helped clean up the doctoring remnants before she waved everyone to the table. "Let's eat. I'm sure everyone's hungry."

A subdued group sat down and passed the food to each other. But after a minute passed, Doug pushed away from the table, his face fixed in a deep frown.

"Doug. Eat first."

"Jean, this has to be dealt with, and I won't be able to rest until it is."

Gordy and Jeff moved to go with him but he waved them to their seats. "No, boys. I'll take care of this."

With obvious hesitation, they eased themselves back into their chairs. Charlie seemed almost ready to say something but Doug cut him off. "Nothing you could have done is a reason to beat you with fencing wire like he did. I won't be long, and this needs taken care of now."

No one at the table appeared happy with their father's decision, but no one was foolish enough to challenge him. Sam was at a loss, but he was certain Gordy's dad could deal with almost anything. It was obvious which parent Gordy got his size from, and it wasn't his mother's family. Everyone watched as he pulled on a pair of heavy work boots and walked out of the door.

"Is Dad going to be okay?" Heather asked.

"Your father will be fine. He can take care of himself," Jean said.

Sam glanced at Gordy's mother. *She is one pissed-off lady.*

* * * *

An hour had passed and the entire family became more apprehensive by the minute. No one was hungry, and after a few weak attempts at getting her family to eat, Jean gave up and they put away the food. The family congregated in the living room while the television no one was watching ran in the background. Jeff had released Charlie's hand from his grip but still hovered closely.

"Dad's home," Heather said as she glanced out the window for the second time in the last minute.

Everyone rushed for the door, but Jean motioned them to stay where they were. "Your dad doesn't need you all hovering around and asking questions." She glanced at her eldest daughter and nodded. "Hannah, get your dad some sweet tea. I'm sure he'll be thirsty."

The door opened, and every eye was riveted on the man who walked through. He seemed none the worse for wear, at least from what Sam could tell. He made his way to his recliner, which he sank into with a sigh. He smiled when someone handed him a glass of tea, which he drained half of before stopping. Then he sat it on the table beside him and fastened his eyes on Charlie and Jeff.

"Your father is a difficult man. I won't pretend to understand his view of life. but I can't abide him beating his children. He made a mistake in reminding me that your eighteenth birthday was a month back. You're welcome to stay here, if you'd like."

Charlie looked like he'd gotten a reprieve from a death sentence—and maybe he had. His gaze darted around the room, waiting for someone to tell him it was a joke. Jeff beamed at him, giving him a reassuring hug.

When they broke their exchange, Doug was studying them.

"There's another talk in our future, isn't there?" Doug asked.

Sam couldn't help a smile creeping across his face and Gordy snorted.

Chapter Seventeen

The scorching late June heat wave made it miserable to be outside, and the tiny air conditioner in Gordy's trailer ran all the time to keep it at a somewhat comfortable temperature. It also meant that they didn't want to do anything that would make the room hotter.

Sam surveyed the contents of their little refrigerator, trying to find something for lunch. *It sounds like Gordy's conversation with his parents is winding down. Tuna. Tuna salad sounds nice and cool. And easy, too. A little Miracle Whip, a spoonful of sweet relish, some chopped onions, and it's done.*

Gordy walked into the front of the trailer with the phone to his ear and grinned at Sam. *Good, another drama-free conversation.*

"Okay, Mom. Love you, too." There was another pause while Gordy nodded. He had Sam grinning when he was doing the 'wrap it up' sign with his finger. "I'll tell Sam. Talk to you soon."

Gordy made sure the call disconnected, laid his phone on the counter and ground his fists against his eyes. "Oh my gosh, I'm glad we're a hundred miles away from the drama at Mom and Dad's house."

"And what were you suppose to tell me?"

"Oh, Mom said the stuff you sent was very helpful. She still doesn't understand the distinction Jeff's making, but she's working on it."

"Yeah, it's sometimes tough for LGBTQ folks, too. Bisexuals are lumped with whoever they're with, so if they're with the opposite sex, they're straight, and if they're with the same sex, they're gay. People don't get it."

"I'm working on it. I thought Jeff fucked anything."

Sam stared at him and lifted an eyebrow. "That's kind of stupid. You know your brother better than that." He paused before shrugging. "I shouldn't come down on you so hard. A few of the people in the GSA on campus explained about being bi. That helped me understand."

Gordy sighed. "I know. I know. It's just that it's...well, Jeff."

"Did you not notice how protective he was of Charlie?"

"Yeah, I noticed. I should at least cut him some slack."

Sam diced the last of the onions and dumped all the ingredients into a bowl. He mixed in the other stuff while Gordy popped several slices of bread into the toaster. A little later they sat at the table and made sandwiches. They'd eaten quietly for a while when Sam's mounting concern forced him to ask, "Did they say anything else about us? That last afternoon was taken up talking to the sheriff and getting Charlie moved into the spare bedroom. I wondered what they were thinking."

Gordy considered for a minute. "They've had so much crap tossed at them that I think a gay son with a boyfriend is the least of their troubles. Charlie's dad will go to jail, and since Charlie isn't a minor, he can stay wherever he wants without needing to involve any courts. Of course, Jeff wants him there, but Mom and Dad aren't thrilled with the live-in boyfriend."

Gordy took another bite of his sandwich and stared into space while he chewed. Once he swallowed, Gordy turned to Sam. "I talked to the people at LGBT Services."

"About?"

"Coming out."

The short answers he was getting were annoying Sam. "Spill it, Gordy. You already told your parents and that went pretty well."

He took a deep breath and let it leak out. "I can't come out on campus. If I don't have my scholarships, I'm screwed. They said that my coming out was mine, and it should happen however I feel the most comfortable. I was lucky with my family, and Hannah still isn't happy."

"Where does that leave us?"

"I think you should live here. We can't be as open as we'd like, but I love you. Once I graduate, the sports scholarships won't matter — whether I go Pro-ball or to grad school." Gordy stopped talking, and the silence became thick as he refused to meet Sam's eyes.

He realized Gordy was waiting for his response, but Sam had been thinking about this and knew his answer. "I've been checking, too, and talking with the LGBT Center Director. She said that coming out is different for each person and just because I was able to tell everyone to fuck off if they didn't like it that doesn't mean it's the same for you. You took a huge chance telling your family and I think it was at least partially because of me. That was amazing. I think keeping your sexuality on the down low with the team isn't unreasonable. I understand that you need your scholarships." He chuckled a little before continuing. "It's not like I can afford to be your sugar daddy."

The tension leaked from Gordy like a bike tire ridden over goathead stickers. A cocky grin grew across his face and he leaned over the table and kissed the tip of Sam's freckled nose. He paused for a moment before easing back to his seat then smiled at Sam. "So, you're up to being my sugar daddy and living here?"

"I said you were too expensive as a rent boy..." Sam became coy. "And, yeah, I'm up to staying here. But what're you going to tell the football team when they ask why you're living with another guy?"

"It's college! They know I'm broke. I need someone to help with expenses."

Sam lifted an eyebrow. "And the sleeping arrangements?"

Gordy shrugged and grinned. "The sleeping arrangements are nobody else's business. They shouldn't be so nosy."

"Yeah, you got nosy friends. What about Nate and Sarah?"

Gordy winked at Sam. "I've already talked to them. They

invited us to dinner."

Sam ate the last of his sandwich and shook his head.

"What?" asked Gordy.

Sam swallowed but paused for a few seconds before speaking. "You better be careful. You're talking about living pretty out for someone who isn't."

Gordy stood up and stepped in front of Sam. "It'll be fine. But about that whole rent-boy thing…"

Sam stared at Gordy's package before licking his lips as he let his gaze travel up his boyfriend's hard body. He stared at Gordy's rugged face and melted inside. The dark scruff of their relaxed weekend made Sam want him all the more. What he really wanted was to jump Gordy and the two of them fuck until they lay gasping for air, but he was afraid he'd have another panic attack. His counseling sessions did seem to be helping, but the whole thing was frustrating as hell.

Gordy moved closer, leaned forward and braced himself with a fist on either side of where Sam was sitting. If he was trying to turn Sam on, he was succeeding. The delicious aroma that was all Gordy left Sam's pulse pounding in his ears and his equipment going stiff. It didn't take long before the crotch of his jeans stretched tight. Gordy moved with gentle deliberation and cupped Sam's face in his hands. He was lightheaded as Gordy kissed his bottom lip, first with tender attention then evolving to passion. Heat flashed over Sam's face and left his ears burning as Gordy eased himself away until Sam focused on the handsome face in front of him.

He stood, wrapped his hands around the back of Gordy's neck, and pulled them together. Sam pressed their lips firmly with a heat that continued to build. Then he tugged at Gordy's shirt until it was untucked, then he dragged it up his lover's chest. As he enjoyed the texture under his hands, he pressed the shirt higher until it popped free and he threw it across the room to land on the window. The expression on Gordy's face matched the lust gathering inside Sam.

Sam shed his shirt and tossed it away. Before it hit the floor, he had put his jeans-covered legs around Gordy's waist and his arms around Gordy's neck. Their eyes met and Sam sensed the moment of passion.

"I want to try again," Sam said.

"Babe, you sure?"

He swallowed hard and gave a quick nod. "Let's try. I really want to try."

Gordy dropped his hands lower and cupped Sam's butt. He stared at Gordy for a moment before grabbing him in an embrace They kissed and their tongues dueled. Gordy ran his hand across Sam's back, sending a tingle through him, and the comfort he experienced was like nothing he'd ever known before.

Their lips parted as they gasped for air and he whispered into Gordy's ear, "Let's go to the bedroom. I want to make use of those clean bills of health we have."

"Ah, fuck," Gordy sighed as he turned and carried Sam to bed. Gordy held Sam against his chest as he eased himself onto the edge and lay down with Sam on top. Sam was finding it so erotic to have their bare chests against each other while from the waist down the denim was sending... interesting sensations through him. He curled down and wriggled the tip of his tongue over Gordy's nipple. When it hardened, he scraped his teeth over it, and reveled in the moan he drew from Gordy.

He realized there was a sense of confinement. He had to do something or it would again go bad. He raised his torso until his forearms were against the broad chest under him. Their eyes met and to Gordy's credit, he understood.

"What? I'm doing something to trigger you."

"I love your hugs..."

Gordy lifted his arms over his head and gave Sam a smile. Sam said, "Thanks, babe. I'm sorry to be—"

Gordy cut him off. "Don't you dare apologize. If we only stay here and cuddle, I'm fine with that."

Sam grabbed his face and shook it playfully. "I don't want to cuddle. My dick's going to fall off from all the damn cuddling."

Gordy choked a little as he tried to keep from laughing but soon both of them were chuckling. Once they'd caught their breath, Sam crawled upward until he hovered above Gordy's chest. It smelled of soap with a tinge of musk, just enough to curl through Sam's senses. Unwilling to resist, Sam buried his nose in the hair in the center of Gordy's chest and inhaled. *Getting high must be like this.* He couldn't imagine anything making him feel more, well…high. He flicked his tongue up and down the fur-lined torso until the hair was curly and wet.

He moved across Gordy's heaving chest until he reached an erect nipple to enjoy the erotic flavors and sensation again. He enjoyed the treasure trove until Gordy was one long, rolling groan. He lay across Gordy, wiped his face and grinned.

"That was fucking hot. What do you want to do now?"

Gordy's wink melted Sam and his voice caught in his throat. Then Gordy grinned. "I've got an idea."

Sam tilted his head and lifted one brow. "What do you have planned, big boy?"

Gordy shifted, tossing Sam to the bed beside him. He reached down, opened his jeans and squirmed out of them. Sam's grin broadened at the sight of Gordy's bare ass.

"Commando?"

Gordy's grinned coyly. "Well, I showered, and underwear seemed a little confining." He crawled onto the bed, lay on his stomach and balled up a pillow to lay his head on. Gordy's hot masculine body had never failed to turn Sam on. This time was no exception.

He wasn't a bulky body builder, but that wasn't Sam's thing. He was big and masculine, but still looked normal. At least what Sam considered normal — and hot. His bare body sprawled across the bed ratcheted up Sam's excitement. The fan of hair that covered each butt cheek to disappear between them was a sight Sam never tired of seeing.

He dropped his hands onto the small of Gordy's back and slipped them as high as he could manage. He held it for a moment before pulling himself away. His breathing deepened as he let himself caress the twin globes of Gordy's ass. The slightly coarse texture sent chills up and down his spine. The blood was also again pumping into his cock until it pressed hard against his jeans.

Unable to resist, he lowered his face and kissed at the join of Gordy's cleft. He groaned, and Sam froze.

Gordy spoke after a moment. "That felt good. Why'd you stop?"

Heat rushed through Sam's skin. "I didn't think you'd want me messing with you like that."

Gordy chuckled. "I strip buck naked, lay down with my ass sticking up and you're worried about touching my butt?"

The heat from Sam's face built until it would have lit sparklers for an Independence Day celebration. He tried to speak several times but kept failing. Gordy's grin was growing with his discomfort.

"Here," Gordy said. "Is this obvious enough?"

He raised to his hands and knees, spread his knees and dropped his chest to the bed. He stared back at Sam, but his breathing was heavier, too. Sam was amazed how sexy Gordy looked in such an exposed pose. His hesitation disappeared at the sight in front of him. When Gordy wiggled his butt and grinned even broader, Sam's last reserve broke. He knelt behind Gordy, opened his cheeks and a surge of desire filled him. Sam planned to fuck Gordy until he couldn't do anything but moan.

He leaned in close and watched, captivated, as Gordy's dusky opening twitched and clenched as if it were drawing Sam in closer. He dipped inward, flicked his tongue against Gordy's hole and lapped over it like an ice cream cone. A growling roar erupted from Gordy as his body shook. "Holy crap! That's amazing."

Sam jumped to his feet, stripping as quickly as possible then moved behind Gordy. He dragged his cockhead along Gordy's crack, coating the length of it with his leakage. After a pass or two, the pre-cum soaked Gordy and left him moaning even louder.

Sam pressed harder each time he slipped across Gordy's opening, his spongy knob dipping inside. The heat and friction was building to an incredible level.

Someone pounded the trailer door like a battering ram. "Hey! What are you doing in there? You invited us to go to Joe's."

Sam and Gordy froze then scrambled around the room. "Fuck, fuck, fuck. It's Nate and Sarah. I forgot we were going out," Gordy said with a hoarse whisper.

"Nate's timing sucks! And not in a good way," Sam said as he struggled to get dressed.

Another flurry of pounding hit the door. "Come on. Get up. We're hungry."

"Hang onto your drawers. We're coming," Gordy yelled as he jumped around trying to put on a sock and shirt at the same time. He yanked the shirt down around his torso and headed toward the door. He glanced at Sam and found him wiggling his feet into a pair of flip-flops. With a welcoming smiled plastered on his face, Gordy swung the door open.

"Sorry, we were taking a nap. But we're up for some cheese fries."

Nate stepped into the trailer with a smirk, even though Sarah tried to keep him out. "Let's wait out here, Nate. They'll be ready in a minute."

Nate slipped an arm around his wife's waist and chuckled. "Oh, it'll take them a little while to wake up from their" — Nate did air quotes with his fingers — "*nap*."

She rolled her eyes but let her husband guide her inside. He plopped into the chair and pulled her into his lap.

"Nathan! Stop that."

"Why? They were getting frisky. It's only fair that I at least get a kiss."

"Nate!" Sarah said.

Gordy tugged on his boots, stood up and wiggled his feet into place. "I'm telling you, we were just resting."

Nate gave Sarah a peck before grinning at Gordy and nodding toward a pair of underwear hanging from the light fixture.

As Sam came from the bedroom where he'd been watching the exchange, Gordy grabbed the underwear and tossed them to Sam. He shot them to the bed and shut the door before turning back with a grin.

"Hey, Sam. How was the nap?" Nate teased.

Sam grinned maliciously. "Excellent, but I couldn't quite get in the rhythm to hit that deep REM like I'd wanted."

Nate roared, and even Sarah grinned at the two of them.

Chapter Eighteen

Sam glanced at his phone and shook his head. No text from Gordy. Practice was going late again. Since the fall workouts had begun a few weeks ago, Gordy seemed more beat-up each day. He was so tired and sore that all he wanted to do was eat supper and fall into bed. He was usually snoring before Sam undressed.

Sam put his workspace into order and smiled when Rachel waved from a few stations away. Sam was at the end of his shift at the campus IT center and was planning to meet Gordy at the stadium. It looked as though Gordy wouldn't be ready for a while.

Rachel startled him when she slapped his back. "Hey, Doherty. How do you like having a real job?"

He chuckled at his friend. "I've worked here for the last couple of semesters. It's not that different being here full-time instead of part-time. Besides, I was the one who got you a job here."

With false shock, she pressed her hand to her chest. "Me? You? I can't believe you'd say that."

Sam rolled his eyes. "Whatever. You're such a troublemaker. But your shift is starting, and I'm outta here."

Rachel stepped closer and said with a wink, "Tell hot stuff I said hi."

The corners of Sam's mouth twitched slightly, but his concern about Gordy filled him. "I'll tell him. Some support would be good. I bet the asshole coach is targeting him."

"You think he knows?"

Sam shrugged but his stomach knotted even tighter. "I'm not sure. But Gordy's been more exhausted than any time

I can remember. We get home and he falls asleep before supper. And Gordy doesn't miss a meal."

She nodded for a minute before motioning him toward the door. "Go rescue hot stuff. But you're right, it seems like we should be able to do something."

"I don't know how to help. But I'll tell Gordy you asked how he was."

Sam slung his book bag over his shoulder and walked through the glass entrance. A few minutes later, he was making his way through the intertwined pathways outside the athletic complex. Usually, he stayed well away from the locker room, but after the last few days, he wanted to spend a little more time with Gordy.

Even as concerned as he was, he didn't want to cause trouble. He found a long concrete bench to the edge of the sidewalk out of the athletics building. He glanced around and saw the area was deserted but thought little about it. Gordy always came out this door. He brought out the textbook for the class he took this semester. His parents weren't very happy that he had delayed graduation, but when he explained he was waiting for Gordy to finish and that he had a full-time job, they were at least mollified for now.

With notes and the textbook surrounding him, he lost himself in the intricacies of another programming language. He didn't notice the footsteps until three guys had positioned themselves around him.

"What's the little faggot doing here?"

Sam raised his head and realized they had him cornered. His stomach knotted and burned. The aching familiarity of this situation had Sam paralyzed for a moment, then he inhaled and let it ease out. Someone besides him would be wiping up blood. He calmed, pulled out his phone and dialed 911. The next instant, the biggest of the three stepped closer and slapped the phone from his hand. Without another word, he lunged at Sam, but Sam's years of martial arts training had him moving on instinct. The hand shot past Sam's chest, missing his grab by inches.

The guy yanked back, his face blood red as he glared at Sam. "You fucking queer! You won't ever want to mess with converting a real man to your perv life again."

"You don't want to do this. They'll throw you out of the university."

Another of the mobile mountains barked out a laugh. "That ain't happening since Coach was the one who told us that you fucked up someone's head, and we should take care of it."

With that news, Sam thought he'd vomit. The problem was, which of the coaches instigated their attack? But he braced himself and made an almost imperceptible shift in his weight to put him in ready stance. The three attackers moved, seeming to believe he was an easy target. Sam hoped they were wrong.

The biggest one charged again, and Sam dodged. Instead of moving away, he redirected the attacker so that he smashed hard against the concrete wall. Blood sprayed and ran between the fingers he clenched against his broken nose. He lifted his blood-drenched hand, glared at Sam and bellowed.

"He broke my fucking nose! Kill him!"

The last two moved together against Sam, and he didn't see a way out. One attacker hesitated for a split second and Sam blocked the grasping hands of the first thug. The two attackers collided and staggered around for a moment. Unfortunately, that gave them time to recover and Sam was facing all three.

His fever grew exponentially at the knife that materialized in the first attacker's hand. Three men after him, one armed. His chances of coming out of this uninjured dwindled, but he'd be damned if he wasn't going to fight until he had nothing left.

Sam prepared himself, locking away the terror. Suddenly, the knife-wielding attacker shot backward like a scene from a Hollywood action flick. He landed several feet away to find Gordy entering into the fray. But as he scrambled, Sam didn't have time to give it more than a passing thought before focusing on the other two.

They moved with more hesitation, giving Sam a few precious seconds to plan before they lunged. He slipped past the first set of grasping hands and with an accurate push, the two brutes entangled with each other. The expressions on their faces should have frightened Sam, but instead, it only made him more determined. He prepared himself when he saw movement to his side. The armed attacker was back. Sam pivoted inward, caught the man's knife hand and redirected the force of his attack.

He was almost at the point where he could put a wristlock on the guy when Gordy did some kind of flying tackle. The force popped Sam's hold loose, and the knife flashed in the late-day sun. Sam dodged but the side of Gordy's jersey parted under its edge like warm butter.

The other two moved to either side with malicious grins. "Stupid faggots. We'll take care of you."

The knife made another swipe, and Sam came close to being cut as he twisted away, but once he'd turned back, a thick arm was tightening around one of the attacker's necks like a huge, dark python. The frantic effort weakened little by little until he went limp.

A rasping sound of someone trying to breathe, along with frantic scrambling boots against concrete from the opposite side, told him Gordy had one of the other attackers. He tasted bile as his need to check on Gordy grew, but the knife-wielding man waited for him to leave an opening. Sam moved as he'd been taught, staying on the balls of his feet as he watched the last attacker and tried to maintain his distance. The tension built, but he had to wait. The guy weighed at least a hundred pounds more than Sam. There was no way to overpower his attacker, but if he waited...

It came. Tension overwhelmed the guy, and he slashed at Sam. The lock-blade knife swept close enough that every one of Sam's senses screamed at him to run. But Sam gritted his teeth and moved with the attack. Long hours of practice slammed him into autopilot as his subconscious took control. The moment arrived, and in the next second, it looked as if the attacker levitated a few feet above the cement. The world stopped for an instant before he slammed into the sidewalk — hard.

Normal time smashed back over the scene and a pain-filled screech echoed down the walkway. A heartbeat later the attacker raced away, clutching his arm to his chest. Sam ran after him, but he was one step into that progress when he heard Gordy.

"Don't. Call the cops. Nate and I have these two."

He nodded, found his phone where it had been batted from his hand and dialed, fighting to keep from hyperventilating, now that it was over. The operator came on the line, and he focused to answer her rapid-fire questions. When she asked if there were injured, he looked again at Gordy's blood-soaked T-shirt and told her yes, but he wasn't certain how badly.

The police arrived, followed a few seconds later by an ambulance. Police cuffed the two attackers and put them into the squad car while another officer interviewed Sam. The EMTs had checked the cut across Gordy's ribs but didn't seem too concerned about the wound. Before they finished with Gordy's interrogation, Sam answered the last of the questions directed at him. The cops had asked several times if he recognized any of the three and he assured them he didn't. But from the length of time they talked to Gordy and Nate, he guessed the cops were getting a very different reply from them.

He wandered over, stood at Gordy's side and rested his hand on his shoulder. The officer interviewing Gordy glanced at him and nodded without missing a beat. He asked Gordy a few more questions then folded his notepad under his arm.

"It looks like a hate crime, but it's not my call. These two aren't talking, but I'm sure they will. They were smart enough to not have any IDs on them, but we feel sure they have a history so we will identify them soon." He shook his head as if dismissing the ideas coming to mind and brought out a few business cards, handing one to each of them. "We should catch the other guy soon. It's usually easy to get the ones in jail to tell us everything, especially when we talk about the number of years they could be there."

"One of them said the coach sent them. Did you get that down?" Sam asked.

The cop looked at them each and his face settled into a sour expression. "We've got that down, but they are refusing to talk any further. Also, we aren't certain which coach they're talking about. It could be anyone."

"Miller. You should check Coach Miller," Sam said.

"I doubt the head defensive coach is behind the thugs who attacked you, but we'll note your concern on the report." He stopped and studied them both for a minute before continuing. "I'd be careful. Sometimes hate crimes bring out the crazies. You don't want to give them targets. Someone wanted to send you a message, at least that's what we're getting from the two we arrested. But beyond that comment, they didn't say anything."

Gordy tensed under Sam's hand. He tightened his grip and gave Gordy an almost imperceptible shake. The tension remained, but it hid in his response. "Thanks for the advice, Officer. We'll keep it in mind."

The police finished questioning everyone and drove off. Once they were out of sight, Gordy let out a long sigh before turning and grabbing Nate in a hug. He released Nate after a second and stared at him with a knowing smile as he held Nate's shoulders. "You saved our bacon. We might not have survived without you."

Sam lifted an eyebrow and considered arguing Gordy's point, but Nate laughed. "You are so full of shit, Hager. Sam was whipping their asses by himself and he'd have left them in broken pieces. But when the one asshole pulled the knife, all bets were off." He shrugged, but gave Sam a wink. "Well, you'd need to hurt them so they don't get back up. It would have gotten messy." The twinkle shone from his dark brown eyes. "So, I guess I was kind of helping the bad guys so you didn't have to break them too much. Sorry about that, man!"

Gordy started laughing and a second later grabbed his side with a grimace. "Okay, no more laughing. The EMT's said I needed to rest or the cut will reopen and I'll need stitches."

Sam eased the sliced shirt open, but the bandage covered the cut. He let it drop and studied Gordy's face. He would never forget the way his world had dropped from under him when he'd seen Gordy's bloody jersey. Sam studied Gordy until he was convinced he would be fine. He leaned closer and pressed his face against the comforting muscle. He might allow himself the space to break down later but kept it confined to the knot in his stomach that drove him close to vomiting. It had been too close—far too close. But they'd gotten through the attack with only the shallow cut on Gordy's side.

Then he remembered their rescuer. Still holding onto Gordy to keep from collapsing, he met Nate's gaze.

"We owe you big time. You saved our butts." Sam couldn't keep his emotions inside any longer. He threw his arms around Nate and hugged him. They stayed that way until Sam uncoiled himself. "I'm serious. We appreciate everything you did today."

Nate dismissed any obligation with a wave of his hand. "Don't sweat it. Gordy and I have each other's backs. Right, Gordy?"

"Absolutely! Since we first met, Nate and I looked out for each other."

Nate spun and trotted back down the ramp, grabbed the bags he and Gordy had dropped when they'd witnessed Sam being attacked. "I got our stuff. We better go or Sarah will kill me. Somehow, she always finds out about stuff like this before she should."

Gordy intertwined his fingers with Sam's. He tensed and glanced at Gordy. "Gordy, what if—"

Gordy cut him off before he uttered another word. "Fuck them. Fuck 'em all. If those guys had been smarter, we might have serious injuries. If I want to hold hands, then by God, I will."

Sam frowned but then shrugged when he glanced to Nate and found him wearing a broad grin.

Chapter Nineteen

A late fall thunderstorm was rolling closer as Gordy sat staring out the library window. He knew the anxiety of having that kind of storm barreling down. The black cloud coming at them didn't bode well, but the thunderstorm at least didn't have them trapped outside and miles from cover while trying to move cattle because they hadn't kept track of the weather.

Lighting fragmented the sky, and a moment later, a rumble washed over them that said the storm was close. As soon as the thought passed through his mind, huge drops of rain splashed against the expanse of glass before him. More lightning slashed across the sky and thunder filled Gordy's ears.

"That's how your stomach sounds when supper is late."

He grinned and stuck out his tongue at Sam. "That just means it likes your cooking."

Sam stretched, his fitted shirt sliding upward until he exposed his flat belly, including the ginger trail that gathered around his navel before plunging downward to disappear into the top of his jeans. Gordy stared until he realized the effect the show was having on him. He wouldn't be standing up soon.

"You are an evil man," he growled at Sam.

Sam smirked and swiveled his hips just a little to tease Gordy further. Sam moved closer and got a sharp slap on his butt. He yelped and Gordy gave him a scowling expression. "Do your homework. You'll get us in trouble."

Sam folded his arms across Gordy's shoulder then leaned in to whisper in his ear, "Are you hard? You want to fuck my pale little ass?"

Gordy growled, not wanting Sam to know just how affected he was and how much he wanted to plow Sam. He was horny enough that what he'd like to do was push Sam onto the table, rip his pants open and ram his cock inside. But then he'd have an unfortunate arrest and jail time for some kind of perverted crimes. Everything was going too well in his private life to screw it up by letting his hormones out to play.

He uncoiled Sam from his neck and lifted him. Gordy thought he'd heard someone moving nearby but when he checked, there was no one else in their remote corner. He pulled Sam onto his lap and gave him a quick kiss. "Behave and I'll make you ecstatic when we get home. But I'd just as soon not be arrested in the library. I mean, gay men having sex in a college bathroom? Do we want to be the cliché?"

Sam grinned at him and wiggled his ass against Gordy's hardness. "But we aren't in the bathroom. There's not even one close."

"Even worse, smart ass." Gordy tried to find something to distract him from Sam's weight on his lap. After several abortive attempts, he remembered a question he'd wanted to ask Sam anyway. "Did you hear from the cops? I hoped they would have caught the guy by now."

With a sigh, Sam stood and made his way back to his chair. "Well, aren't you the little mood killer." He scowled at Gordy.

"That was the whole idea. But I want to know, too."

Sam plopped in his seat, stared at Gordy for a minute then shook his head. "You're your own biggest cock blocker. Do you know that?"

Gordy grinned. "You're just horny and thinking with the little head."

Sam rolled his eyes, but Gordy resisted the cute behavior. Sam sighed in acceptance and stared through the window for a minute at the still building storm. "It looks bad. Do you think it could be tornadoes?"

"You're stalling. Answer my question."

"Fine. Someone hired them to beat me up, but they don't have names or much else. They were looking for roughneck work and the guy paid them a buttload of cash to make sure I got the message that the gays aren't welcome."

"The gays?"

"Yeah, lovely, isn't it?"

"Nice. What about the guy with the knife?"

"He was someone hitching a ride with them. He must have had enough cash for gas, which they didn't. But no one has spotted him since he attacked us."

Gordy shook his head. He didn't like how the cops were treating them but didn't know what to do about it. When he glanced at Sam, it was obvious neither of them was in the mood for any more studying. He put things back in his book bag then looked at Sam. "Let's get home and have some fun."

Books started flying as Sam tossed everything inside, slung it over one shoulder then headed for the door. A few steps later he glanced back at Gordy. "What's taking you so long?"

* * * *

Tension built inside Sam with each mile they traveled closer to the trailer. His nerves knotted and unknotted as his desire for Gordy built. There had been enough fooling around. He was ready to fuck. It had been at least a week since either of them had relieved their building steam. He looked over to Gordy and smiled. His hot tackle boyfriend was flushed and Sam was certain there was a bulge in his crotch.

Our clothes are getting wrecked, again.

Sam pressed his back against the seat, fighting with his hormone-filled body and now-urgent dick. What he wanted more than anything was to unzip Gordy's jeans, fish his cock out and suck on it like a frozen pop in the heat of summer. But it would change to a wet and sticky mess in no time.

Gordy swung into the driveway and the sound of gravel crunching under the deep tread of his pickup welcomed them home. They parked outside the tiny trailer and sat with neither of them looking at the other as they stared through the windshield. "I'm so horny that it's unbelievable. It's been too long, and you are so fucking hot."

A deep throaty chuckle leaked from Sam. "If we don't go inside right now, I'm not responsible for what happens."

"Yeah. Got it. Me, too."

They bailed from the truck, and while Sam was certain they were both trying to be calm, it was best that no one was around to see them. They burst through the door and turned on each other as soon as the door shut. Sam grabbed Gordy's face between his hands and pulled him into a passionate kiss while grinding against his lover. Their lips pressed together hard as they twisted and turned, battling the flood of desire flowing between them.

Sam slipped his tongue between Gordy's lips and drove inside. Gordy met his advance with an equal amount of fervor. The heat in Sam continued to build until his control stretched thin. As he pulled away, he tilted Gordy's head back and etched a path from the base of his neck to his square chin. He stopped then ran his tongue inside Gordy's mouth.

Gordy stared at him for a moment before tilting his head. "Something wrong?"

"You have a heavy fucking beard. Feels different against my tongue."

"Is that bad?"

Sam considered for a moment. "No. Just hadn't noticed it before."

"Are we done talking?"

Sam grinned. "Yeah. I'm finished."

Gordy grabbed Sam, and with one effortless move, threw him over his shoulder and walked to the bedroom.

It shocked Sam into silence for a second before he twisted and tried to break loose. "Hey! Who do you think you are? Tarzan or something?"

"Sam talks too much. Sam need be quiet so not get dropped."

He giggled then slapped a hand over his mouth. He wasn't sure where that sound came from, but it wasn't one he wanted to make before having sex with a college football hero. His attention came away from whatever was on his mind when Gordy slipped his huge hand under the waistband of Sam's jeans and rubbed across his ass. The attention had its desired effect on Sam and his dick throbbed.

Gordy brought him around so their chests were smashed against each other and leaned in for another kiss. Sam wrapped his legs around Gordy and held on tightly. He grabbed Gordy's rough face and kissed him hard. Sam was grinding against Gordy, kissing with enough passion to keep them warm all winter, when Gordy yelped.

He pulled back as Gordy ran his tongue over his teeth. A second later, he smiled. "Easy there, stud. I'd like to have front teeth left once we're finished. Avoiding at least some of the redneck look would be great."

Sam grinned and lunged for a quick nip on the side of Gordy's neck. "It's a deal. I'll do my damnedest to not knock out any teeth. You just make me so fucking horny."

Desire washed over Sam, and he unbuttoned Gordy's shirt. Once he opened the last button, he let the fabric drop open and admired Gordy's torso for several delicious moments. The dark hair swept down each side of his muscular chest, accenting his large brown nipples. Sam leaned forward, scraping his teeth along one of them. Once the sounds coming from Gordy were loud enough to be heard outside, Sam changed his tactics. He flicked his tongue over the now-hard nub of flesh until Gordy was moaning even louder. He moved away, enjoying the ecstasy etched across Gordy's square face as he rubbed his thumb over both nipples.

"How's that? Should I quit?"

Gordy stared at Sam through slitted eyes, his lips in a smirk. "If you don't finish what you started, you'll be beating off in the shower for a long time."

"So, maybe I should finish?"

"Yeah, might be a good plan."

Sam chuckled but slipped Gordy's shirt from his shoulders and let it flutter to the ground. He repeated his attention to Gordy's other nipple until he had both of them jutting hard above the hair surrounding them. Sam planted kisses down the center of his chest, enjoying Gordy's slightly rounded belly. He knelt before Gordy, licking his way through the hair surrounding Gordy's navel before he pressed his face into his crotch. Sam inhaled deeply, the strong musk filling his system and making his cock jerk in his pants. He gnawed at the lump he found until Gordy forced him upward.

He wiped across his face but Gordy took the tail of his shirt and wrenched it off, tossing it into the corner. Sam grinned as Gordy grabbed him under his arms and tossed him onto the bed. Gordy taking charge thrilled Sam like never before. Gordy crawled between Sam's legs, twisted down and gnawed on Sam's shaft for a moment. They were panting from the level of excitement when Gordy reached up and unbuttoned Sam's jeans until his briefs were bulging through the opening. Gordy looked hungrily at Sam.

"You ready?"

Sam trembled, his body filled with desire for Gordy. A look passed between them, and Sam nodded. Gordy grabbed Sam's clothes and worked them down. The cool air caressed Sam's bare skin as more became exposed. His pubic hair came into view, as did the root of his cock. The pressure and thrill of Gordy discovering him amped the attraction as never before. Gordy tugged again, and the clothing shot free. Sam's cock escaped its confines to arc across his crotch, trailing a thin translucent strand. A second later, Gordy finished stripping Sam and drank in the naked form before him. When their eyes met, Gordy grinned and stripped.

"Fuck, you are *so* hot," Gordy said as he kicked the wad of clothing off his feet. Without hesitation, Gordy crawled between Sam's legs. He leaned close to kiss the inside of Sam's thigh then take his cockhead into his mouth. The wet heat, followed by friction from Gordy's tongue as he flicked into the loose skin gathered at its crown, sent pleasure boiling through Sam like a summer wild fire. He didn't think his lust could build any further when Gordy grabbed the base of his cock and stroked it while his tongue dug into the ample foreskin. The combination built until the familiar sensation washed over him.

Too soon. Not yet.

He grabbed at Gordy until he moved higher, their crotches grinding against each other. He grabbed the sides of Gordy's head and pulled him into a kiss. "I'm about to shoot. I don't want to lose it already."

Gordy was panting, his gasps filled the room and he looked desperate with need. As the moment cooled, Gordy became more coherent. "What do you want? I'm up for anything," Gordy said.

Sam's lust was begging, but he wasn't sure what his macho football player would think about his choice. His concern must have telegraphed to his expression.

"What's wrong?" Gordy asked.

"Nothing. Let's go back to what we were doing."

"I think you're full of crap. Tell me what you want? I'm open to anything."

"Gordy…"

"Spit it out, stud."

"Really, let's forget about it."

The expression on Gordy's face said it all.

"Okay, but I told you it was a bad idea. It'd be hot to top you," Sam said.

The instant the words left his lips, he wished he hadn't said them. He knew Gordy would be offended. *Now what am I going to do? I won't lose Gordy over something like sex.*

"Yeah, that sounds hot."

Shock rippled through Sam, and he met the big man's gaze. "Honest? With me?"

"Well, there's no one else around I want to have sex with, so yeah, you. Besides, I'd already told you that it would be hot to bottom for you. I think I was pretty much begging for it when Nate and Sarah showed up and that didn't happen."

"Fuck. I completely forgot." Sam sat still, trying to take in the moments. This was his fantasy come true, and Gordy seemed equally excited. He caressed Gordy's cheek, losing himself in the deep brown eyes. "How do you want to do this? It's not like I'm an expert at it."

"Get the bottle of lube. You'll need to get me ready. I'd like to sit down without wincing tomorrow, so we're not going to rush."

Sam crawled to the edge of the bed to retrieve the bottle stored in the side table. Once he turned, Gordy moved so he was face down with his round butt in the air. He turned and grinned at Sam. "Take it slow and use a ton of lube. Start with one finger up there. We'll see how things go."

Sam nodded and drenched Gordy's cleft with lube. The clear liquid eased lower until Sam caught it with a finger and covered the spots that weren't coated. He worked it into Gordy with more of his finger disappearing with each pass. Soon, he slipped inside to the first knuckle and the sounds from Gordy were building. Sam pulled almost out, added more lube then pushed back inside, making his finger disappear. After giving Gordy time to get used to the intrusion, he began little thrusts. Then he hit Gordy's prostate, and Sam thought he'd be tossed like an amateur bull rider. The noise Gordy made wasn't too much less than one of the huge bulls his family had on their ranch. He targeted the magic spot and Gordy broke into whimpers.

Sam let his finger slide out and readied two fingers. He guided them in, waiting each time it seemed Gordy needed to adjust. But with patience, he soon eased the digits inside Gordy. After he repeated the process with a third finger, Gordy was a quivering mass of muscle. Sam couldn't resist the hot, round ass in front of him.

He squirted three thick lines of lube down his cock then stroked until it was coated. Sam did the same to Gordy's ass. He tossed the bottle to one side and moved into position. Sam grabbed his hard cock and ran it up and down Gordy's lube-soaked crack until everything was ready. He found the opening and pressed against it. The tight muscles gave way to the constant pressure. Sam paused when a long, loud groan came from Gordy.

"You okay? We can stop," Sam said.

"Don't you dare. This is the best thing I've ever done. Your dick's a perfect fit."

Sam pushed again, and he slipped past the final barrier. He grabbed Gordy's waist and wedged himself inside. In no time, Sam ground his crotch against Gordy's ass. The taut heat made Sam want to pound Gordy, but he held back with only the greatest of willpower. When the muscles clenched around his hard dick lessened, Sam pulled back a little then pushed forward.

"Oh shit. That's damn amazing. Fuck me, Sam."

Sam pumped himself inside as the room filled with their intimacy and heat. The strokes became hard and quick as they moved together. His crotch tightened and Sam knew his climax was close. He reached around Gordy and played with his nipples while he gave a rapid-fire series of thrusts he hoped was leaving Gordy's prostate primed. Then the wave of euphoria washed over him and he buried himself deep inside and trembled. It began and his body convulsed again and again as he emptied himself. As the final wave washed over him, he collapsed. Sam panted as he twisted to kiss Gordy's sweat-dampened neck and dropped his head against Gordy. "That was amazing. I've never had anything that good. Maybe I could stay here forever."

"It was amazing, and I feel fantastic."

Sam lay still for a moment before sliding his hand down Gordy's stomach to find his hard cock. He squeezed it and whispered, "Roll over and I'll make it even better."

There was no discussion, and a moment later, Gordy was on his back with his thick cock jutting from his crotch. Sam curled beside him and wrapped his fingers around Gordy's dick. He stroked it a few times before moving closer, running his tongue up its length, then swirled it around the swollen head. The musky flavor filled Sam's senses as Gordy leaked out pre-cum.

"Fuck! I'm not gonna last long if you keep that up."

Sam sank his mouth over Gordy's cock and pumped it into his throat. Once Gordy was thrashing on the bed from Sam's oral skills, he reached back and sank his finger deep inside Gordy. Unable to speak, Gordy twisted and groaned as Sam worked to take him closer to the edge. The combination worked its magic, and within a minute, he had Gordy tensing.

"Gonna come!"

To his surprise, Sam found himself eager to take the load. He wrapped his lips around Gordy's cock and pressed his finger deep inside. He sensed the first convulsion pass through Gordy and his mouth filled with a masculine essence. Sam swallowed again and again as Gordy emptied his balls. Gordy slid his fingers through his hair, but Sam was grateful Gordy didn't hold his head. The exchange continued for what seemed like several minutes before Gordy collapsed against the bed, gasping. Sam nursed the last drops from Gordy before curling against him. When he exchanged a kiss with Gordy, he grinned at Sam.

"What's so funny?" Sam asked.

"Your kiss tasted like cum."

"And you have a problem with that?"

"Not at all. Best protein shake I've ever had."

Sam chuckled and winked at Gordy. "Next time, we'll see how you like my private mix."

"I'd like that." As they exchanged another kiss, Gordy's

phone buzzed, signaling a text message. Gordy frowned. "Who could that be?"

Sam traced a finger along Gordy's jaw and chuckled. "Look at your phone. You know it's going to make you crazy until you do."

Gordy scooted to the side of the bed and grabbed the phone. "What the hell?"

"What?"

"Coach Miller wants to see me."

Chapter Twenty

Gordy stood outside the coach's office, wondering what was wrong. Coach Miller didn't give players a break if they messed up. He hoped this wasn't one of those times, but he had no idea why the coach asked to meet with him. The only thing he could think of was he and Sam, but they'd been so careful. Gordy had arrived on time to find a note with instruction to wait.

He'd been at Miller's office for several minutes and the tension wore on his nerves. It didn't help that Sam had freaked out, too. He hadn't slept all night because he'd worried about Gordy. He'd tried to calm Sam, but he wasn't at his best at three a.m. Sam had left at first light and gone back to his dorm room. His pretense was to give Gordy a few hours to relax himself, but Gordy thought it was to keep them from fighting and adding to his tension. Gordy wasn't sure it had helped, but he didn't want to waste energy debating about it at this point. Just when his nerves had shredded, the door opened and the head coach walked out.

The head coach stopped and locked gazes with the defensive coach. "This can't be allowed to happen. I won't permit that kind of behavior. This university has standards, and we can't let this happen."

"I agree, Mark. Keep an eye open for anything. It's a serious problem. You're right. We have to deal with the issue as soon as we discover it."

"It's outrageous we are still dealing with it. It needed eradicated long ago." The head coach turned and Gordy wished he could have been anywhere else. After the exchange he'd overheard, he had no doubt why he'd been called in. His secret was out, and he built toward a full panic. He considered running until he collapsed, but that wasn't an option. He needed his degree and intended to finish. He realized Coach Torres was talking to him.

"Nice job last weekend, Hager. Now, don't do something stupid to jeopardize everything you've worked toward." The head coach spun on his heel and was halfway down the hall before Gordy collected his thoughts.

"Get in here, Hager."

He found the coach scowling at him from the open door. Gordy walked past him and sank into the chair opposite his massive desk. Gordy glanced up once, saw the coach's hard expression and dropped his eyes to his feet. Then it all began with no preamble.

"We have a serious problem, and you know what I'm talking about. Coach Torres and I were discussing your issues. I'll be honest. Anyone else caught at this and they'd already have been on their way home. But you're a good team player, so we're willing to give you a chance to fix it. But I'll tell you that I had to work hard to keep you on this team. Coach Torres wanted you out."

Gordy's throat constricted as the statement washed over him. *Maybe I'm wrong? I can't lose Sam. I can't. But I have to finish my degree.* He moved his head in a weak nod and swallowed without choking. But the words wouldn't emerge.

Coach stared for a long time before he spoke again. By then, tense knots filled Gordy's stomach until he came close to puking. "I saw you with that redhaired kid after practice then later in the library." He stopped and sighed. "Where was your head? What if it'd been someone else to see you? You could have destroyed a potential career. Did you not consider that?"

Gordy squeezed out the words. "No, sir. I didn't think about it. It just sort of happened."

Coach's expression left no room for discussion. "You've

chosen a twisted and sinful lifestyle. There's no room on this football team for someone like that. But if you can keep your base desires under control, you can stay. If you return to your unnatural ways, you'll leave the team. You'll be done—out of college."

Gordy blanched. He swallowed hard several times before replying. "But, Coach—"

The coach cut him off with a slash of his hand. "This isn't a discussion. Break off relations with that boy or you won't be on this team any longer. If the other players found out, they'd demand you be thrown off the team. Nobody wants to play with a fag. You have a choice, and I hope at this point you understand what the right choice is."

Stunned, Gordy's world shattered as his biggest fear unfolded. He glanced at the coach's hard face and it was obvious he had no choice. Almost unable to walk, Gordy stumbled out the door. He knew what was next. It was time for him to man-up and talk to Sam.

* * * *

Sam glanced up from the book he was reading when he heard a soft knock at his door. One of his suitemates must have let someone into their shared space. He stared at the door for a few seconds, trying to think who it might be. It couldn't be Gordy. His meeting with Miller had only been going on for a few minutes. Then the knocking started again. He moved into action. He crawled off the bed, took a moment to adjust his clothes then made his way to the door. He was surprised to find Gordy standing there when he opened it.

A smile covered his face at the sight of his boyfriend. "Hey! How are you? What happened to your meeting?" He leaned in to hug Gordy, but Gordy stepped away and Sam filled with dread.

"We need to talk," Gordy said.

Sam motioned him inside. "Sure. Come in."

Gordy pulled out the almost-never-used chair and sat on its hard-plastic seat. Sam dropped onto the bed facing him with apprehension growing every second. A glance at Gordy's face only increased Sam's growing tension. He waited, trying to give Gordy the time he needed to speak. If it were anyone else sitting across from him, he would have thought they were close to tears.

Gordy scrubbed his hand across his face. His expression was like someone with a death sentence. "I can't see you anymore."

Sam came close to hyperventilating, his muscles knotting as he struggled to understand. "Why? Everything seemed to be going great. Why are you breaking up with me?" Sam considered possible reasons before his insecurities crashed over him. He leaned forward and whispered, "Was it something I did?"

The laugh from Gordy was harsh. "You're an innocent bystander. I messed up. I never should have believed I deserved a normal life, not with how I am."

Sam scowled for a minute before turning back to Gordy. "You mean about you being gay? Is that what this is all about? I told you it would be fine. We've been careful. I get that you have to wait until after you graduate."

Gordy shook his head, his expression one of complete dejection. "They found out. Coach Miller saw us in the library and after practice that time. He talked Coach Torres out of kicking me off the team, but they don't want people like me playing college football."

Anger replaced the dejection the more Sam considered what Gordy was telling him. "You mean like you — a genius and a kick-ass football player? That kind of person? Besides, they can't do that. It's against the university's diversity policy. No way can they kick you off the team for being gay. If they were smart, they'd have the whole university public relations department talking to you and sending out press releases by the boxful. This is insane."

"Even if it is against policy, the other players would never agree to be on a team with a gay guy." He looked at Sam and tears were rolling down his face. "He called me a fag, Sam. I don't know. I'm not strong enough to do this."

Sam's head swam as he tried to process what Gordy was telling him, but something didn't fit. It seemed too easy with the weight of the responsibility against Gordy.

"Okay, something's wrong here. Wait to decide until we talk about it."

Gordy lunged to his feet, yelling. "No! Don't make this even more miserable. I can't do this anymore. I can't take it." Sam sat stunned as Gordy raced from the room.

* * * *

Nate paced the floor while Gordy sat with his head between his hands as dejected as he had been at any point in his life. Sarah stopped pretending she was cooking and settled at the table, watching the interaction between the two of them. Nate spun toward Gordy.

"Miller told you he was throwing you off the team because you're gay?"

"He never said I was gay, not exactly. He's seen Sam and I together, like I told you."

"No way. No fucking way! He can't do that. We need to talk with Coach Torres. He won't let Miller get away with it. He's always been good about diversity issues. I bet he'll throw Miller out on his ear."

Gordy's life had gone to shit, and he didn't understand how to save any of it. There was no compromise where he didn't lose something important. He shook himself and tried to focus on Nate's questions. "Torres won't do anything. He was coming out of Miller's office when I got there. From what I overheard, Miller is supposed to deal with me so Torres doesn't have to. He said I've got one chance. Break up with Sam, or I'm off the team and no more scholarship."

The angry storm on Nate's face would have had most

people afraid for their lives. "That's bullshit. You're like their poster child—a top athlete who's an honor student. This would be a PR disaster for State. There's no way they would do it."

"That's what Sam said, too. Coach said the other players would refuse to play if I stayed."

Nate started to argue but sank back into his chair. The room became so quiet that their breathing sounded like a roar. Nate and Gordy's worlds were devastated. Sarah looked at each of them and her scowl worsened.

"Nate? Is that true? Would the other players refuse to play if Gordy was on the team and they knew he was gay?"

Gordy lifted his head, wondering what Nate would say. The longer the silence stretched out, the less hope Gordy had. When Nate began to speak, it was obvious he was uncertain at a level he'd rarely seen from Nate.

"I wish I could say they would be furious that anyone would consider taking Gordy off the team because he's gay. But the truth is that I'm not sure how they'd respond."

"How can you not know? Don't you guys talk about stuff?" Sarah asked.

Nate let out a laugh devoid of humor. "We talk. We talk all the time. But it's not like I would say 'hey, Gordy's gay. That isn't an issue for anyone, is it?' That conversation never happened. And college football doesn't have the best reputation for being accepting."

She stared at him before shaking her head. "This is all stupid. They can't do this to Gordy." She turned to him. "What did Sam say? He knows all the diversity stuff that goes on around this campus. I bet he had ideas."

"Sam told me it was fixable. Y'all don't get it. The coaches don't want me and the other players won't work with me anymore. No one can help me. The university talking heads might come on television and talk about diversity, but if they won't let me play, then it will all go away, anyway. There'd be a bunch of photo ops for a month or so, then I'd be cut from the team because my performance wasn't at the quality it should be to play at this level."

"Gordy —"

He jerked to his feet, overwhelmed and devastated. "I gotta go. Don't say anything, okay? I know my responsibility. I don't want to talk about it anymore. It doesn't make it any easier. It's making me feel like crap."

"I'd feel better if you'd spend the night. I don't want you to be alone tonight," Sarah said.

He studied Sarah until he realized what concerned her. His blank expression transformed into more of a scowl. "I'm not going to do something like try to hurt myself."

"You don't see a problem, but it's not three in the morning and you've been running bad thoughts through your head all night. For me. Please."

Nate nodded. "It happened to one of her cousins when we were dating. It was horrible. Do me a favor and spend the night. We promise to feed you lots of your favorites."

"I'll warm up the tamales we made — with a fresh batch of salsa verde," she said.

"Hey, man. You can't turn that down. You love her tamales. Then tomorrow morning we can go to the gym and work out until you're a lump of goo. It'll all be good."

Gordy threw up his hands in surrender. "Okay! I give up already. But I plan on eating every bite of food in your entire house."

Sarah beamed before making her way to the fridge for homemade hummus and a bowl of pita chips, all of which she set in front of Gordy.

"Get busy eating. I've got plenty more to keep you busy while I get the tamales ready."

Chapter Twenty-One

Sam spent several hours pacing his room as he tried to bring in all the pieces of this disaster. *It's the twenty-first century. No one's going to be thrown off a college sports team for being gay. What do I need to do to fix this?* Once more, something had happened to screw up his and Gordy's lives. Well, he wasn't going to let it pass without putting up one hell of a fight. He'd already learned he was capable of defending himself physically, and he was going to fight for Gordy and he had no intentions of losing. He knew he needed some help on this. He was so furious that someone would do this to Gordy that he couldn't work out a strategy to knock the damn rust off the gears that made change happen around this place.

He abruptly threw himself onto the bed and lay staring at the ceiling while his mind ran a thousand miles a second. He needed desperately to find a solution, and he couldn't even find a starting point. But he knew one thing for certain. He wouldn't lose Gordy, not over this.

"Hey, Red. What's going on? I ran into one of your roomies and he said you and stud muffin had a fight." She grinned at Sam. "What did I tell you about fighting with a man who's almost twice as big as you?"

Sam rocketed off the bed to the sight of Rachel leaning through the door he'd forgot to shut. "Rach! Yes! You're the one I need. Get your ass in here!" Sam grabbed Rachel by the arm and pulled her onto the bed.

He paused for a second to try and tame the chaos going on in his head. Once he could focus, he started trying to explain what had happened but it came out as a mass of barely related words.

"Gordy tried to break-up with me, but that shit isn't happening. They can't throw him off the team because he's gay, and I don't give a shit how pissed off the Neanderthals from the team might be, because a queer is better than they are. It just fuck'n sucks to be them."

Sam stopped to catch his breath and Rachel slapped a hand over his mouth. "Hang on. Hang on. Gordy's getting thrown off the football team because he's gay? They can't do that! And why'd he break up with you?"

Sam pulled her hands away from his mouth and took up where he left off. "Exactly! The assholes *can't* do that! I don't care what the good ole boy's club thinks about their precious pointy ball. Apparently, they told him if he'd butch it up and get rid of the gay arm candy" — he glanced at Rachel — "that'd be me — then they'd keep it all hush hush and let him stay on their precious team."

Now it was Rachel's turn to pace. "This is *not* going to happen. No way. They can't pull this kind of crap on people." She stopped in mid-stride. "Christina. That's who we need to talk with. She's the diversity VP. She'll boil their butts in hot oil. Oh, it will be impressive. Just wait and see. She'll chew them up into tiny pieces and spit them out. Those football boys won't know what hit them. Oh yeah." Rachel was practically rubbing her hands in glee as she planned the battle. She turned to Sam.

"Who else? What'd we need to cover besides the whole homophobia and bigotry side of this? The college newspaper? Should we spill the goods on the whole prejudiced athletics program?"

Sam considered for a minute and thought about the question carefully. He wasn't in the mood to protect the university, but he also didn't want to hurt innocent people. He began to shake his head slowly. "Not yet. It looks like a whole lot of people screwed up, but at least some of it might be a misunderstanding. We can always open that can of shit later if people get more concerned with covering their asses than protecting Gordy."

"Okay, no journalistic orgy — for now. Who else?"

Sam sat for a moment, trying to think who should be brought into the mix. The answer popped into his mind, and Sam grinned at Rachel. "Nate. That's who else we need. He'll fight the coaches and players, especially the players. Gordy was certain none of the team members would tolerate a gay man on the team. I don't think Gordy is giving them credit, but they are the big variable. Nate could get them onboard."

Rachel chewed on her bottom lip for a few moments. But when a smile stretched across her face, Sam knew things were going to be fine. "Good. Let's get going. Gordy's going to be having a meltdown because, bless his heart, he may be a genius, but sometimes he doesn't understand people as well as he thinks."

Her grin had only grown as they talked about it. "Okay. I'm going to the Diversity Office right now. You find Nate and get him onboard. Nothing happens fast at this place, but I don't think they're going to mess around."

Sam considered for a minute or two before looking up. "I'm going to make some phone calls, too. I think there are a few people who would want to know what's happening."

His gaze met Rachel's and they both rushed out of Sam's dorm room.

* * * *

Gordy had situated himself in the darkest part of the library and tried to concentrate on his homework. The past day had been the most miserable he'd ever experienced. Losing Sam had left him with an ache. With each passing hour, he questioned his choices. There had to be another way. He couldn't find it right now, though, and after the way he'd treated Sam, his former boyfriend would never speak to him again.

Gordy tried to focus on the formulas. Tomorrow's exam

was a third of his grade and the only thing that would make this whole situation worse was if his grades dropped. With a fierce scowl, he plunged into his notes again.

He'd lost himself in the work he was doing until a touch on his shoulder jolted him. He twisted to find Nate standing beside him. "Oh my God, you scared the crap out of me. What are you doing up here? I'm surprised you knew where the library was."

Nate popped Gordy on the back of his head. "Don't be a wise ass. Just because the rest of us don't live here doesn't mean we can't find the place."

He studied Nate and tilted his head. "You still didn't answer my question. What are you doing? There's no way you happened to stroll through the least-used part of the library."

Nate became hesitant. "You need to come with me. The coach told me to find you."

"Miller? Why? I didn't do anything wrong."

"No, Coach Torres. He told me to get you and bring you to the Athletic Director's office."

Gordy's stomach sank, and he thought he was going to hurl. "I did what they said to do. I swear, Nate."

Nate grabbed his shoulder and gave him a brotherly squeeze. "Come on, Gordy. It might be okay. Isn't it about time for you to catch a break and for some people to help you?"

He looked at Nate and shook his head. "The way this week's going, I can't expect any help. But whatever. It's not much fun but I guess I'll go talk with Coach Torres and the AD." He packed up his books then threw the backpack over his shoulder while Nate waited. They were closing the distance at a fast walk when he turned to Nate. "You don't need to escort me. I promise I won't run away or do something stupid."

"I'm not leaving you. I'll be waiting outside once you're done."

He smiled at Nate but remained silent as they made their

way across campus. Nate was good to his word once they arrived. Nate talked to the secretary for a minute then came back to sit beside him. He started to say something to Nate when the door shot open and Coach Torres filled the doorway. He spotted Gordy and motioned to him.

"Thanks for coming over on such short notice, Gordy. Dr. Phillips and I decided we shouldn't wait to talk with you. Come back to the conference room."

Gordy's stomach roiled as though he were on the worst carnival ride ever and only seconds from losing his lunch. He followed the coach to an open door. As he stepped in the room, he saw more people seated around a huge, wooden table. The setting increased his anxiety, which he didn't believe was possible. A woman leaned forward and gave him a warm smile.

"Hi, Gordy, I'm Christina, the Vice President of Diversity on this campus. This all must seem pretty intimidating, which isn't our intent. We've received information, and if it's correct, we will take care of the situation immediately."

Gordy was confused. Why would someone from the diversity office want to talk with him? He glanced around the room to find similar expressions of concern, even from Coach Torres. Not knowing what else to do, he turned to Christina. "I haven't done anything that Coach Miller warned me not to do."

The room's atmosphere changed, but not in ways he expected. Most of the expressions he'd label as being filled with sadness. Christina's expression was easy enough to interpret. She was furious.

"Gordy, I apologize for not explaining earlier. This is not a disciplinary meeting. There is nothing you've done wrong. But we are very concerned about discrimination against you. That behavior should never have taken place on this campus."

He sat stunned before he turned to Coach Torres. "I'm not off the team?"

"No, Gordy, not at all. You're a role model for your

teammates. We don't want you to feel you aren't welcome."

"But I'm gay. You told Coach Miller to get rid of the freaks on the team when I was standing there."

The coach stared at Gordy before the realization dawned. "We weren't talking about you, Gordy. A few players have drinking problems. I was telling Coach Miller they had no chances left."

"He said…" Gordy began.

"Gordy, whatever Miller told you was from his imagination. You're one of the best defensive players on this team and by far the best student. We'd never ask you to leave."

This whole conversation left Gordy a little lightheaded. Everyone seemed to smile again. The door opened and closed without Gordy taking note until he realized someone was standing on either side of him. He glanced around and found it was Sam and Nate.

"What's going on? I thought everything was over."

Nate punched him lightly on the arm. "You've done everything you could do. You needed someone else to fix this for you. That's why Sam and I stepped into this mess."

He looked from one of them to the other, but then focused on Sam. "You tried to help me? After what I did?"

Sam chuckled then spouted off. "Of course, you goof. That's what you do when you love someone."

Both Gordy and Sam's face turned brilliant red at Sam's declaration. Gordy glanced around the room and the general reaction was smiles. He found Sam had gone from appearing like a freshly boiled crawfish to pale as snow. And the snow might have more color.

Sam motioned to Gordy and shook his head. "I'm so sorry, Gordy. I shouldn't have said that. My timing sucks. Please don't say anything."

Nate leaned in and tapped Sam on the shoulder. "You'll need lots of flowers and chocolate. I'll give you a list of my suppliers."

This time the smiles became more exuberant. Once the

chuckles had subsided, Christina explained, "Sam and Rachel came to talk about the comments made to you. They were very upset, and when I'd heard the entire story, I was furious. I called Coach Torres, and the incident offended him as much as it had me."

The coach took over the conversation. "Nate showed up to defend you shortly after I spoke with Christina. It didn't take a genius to figure out that Gordy was gay, and everyone had bad information."

Gordy stared at Nate in disbelief and betrayal filled him. "What did you do? We've always had each other's backs. Now you out me to the coach and the whole team?"

Nate dropped his eyes and tightened his lips. But before he responded, Torres interrupted. "He did the right thing. I needed to understand what was happening. This is serious. No one at this university should ever be discriminated against because of their sexual identity. I wish you'd told me a long time ago, and we could've helped. I'm sure this hasn't helping your stress level."

Gordy studied the people in the room, especially his best friend and the man he loved. But they hadn't addressed his last concern. He faced the coach, took a deep breath and asked what worried him the most. "What about the rest of the team? Miller said no one would want to be on a team with a gay guy. And Nate couldn't even say he was wrong."

Nate slung his backpack from his shoulder and dug inside. A few seconds later, he pulled out a thick manila envelope. He grinned at Gordy as he handed the packet to the coach. "It's stuff from everyone on the team saying they want Gordy. There's a letter they signed and a bunch of personal notes." He turned to Gordy with a smirk. "Some of them are pissed that you didn't tell them. They think you didn't trust them. I'm guessing you'll need to invite them to a burger cookout to make up."

Gordy cocked his eye at Nate. "Everyone? Every single backwoods redneck on that team?"

"The country boys on the team are all behind you. They

may ask stupid questions, but it's like they can ask the dumb questions but God help anyone else who messes with you."

"Come on, Nate. A few of them didn't like me before they found out I like dudes. Now…? Well, I can imagine some of their comments."

"Okay. Fine. A few of them are still living in the eighteen hundreds. But they are the same idiots who believe Sarah and I shouldn't be married, so that's just stupid."

Gordy stood wavering between disbelief and relief. He wanted to sit down but was afraid if he did, he'd end up a pool of goo on the floor. He pulled his gaze up again, this time back to Christina. "What will I do about working with Coach Miller? He's not going to be happy."

She glanced to one of the suits that had been silent since he'd arrived and she got a nod. With a vindictive expression, she filled Gordy in with what had happened. "We will escort Coach Miller from the university. He no longer has a job here. He's also being investigated regarding his involvement with the men who attacked you and Sam. That case is active. But regardless, one of the assistant coaches will take over, and you'll not need to deal with him again."

He turned to Sam and worry filled him. "How are we? I seem to be wrong about everything you told me."

Sam smiled, leaned in and kissed Gordy. His typical response of horror and panic flooded him, but then the realization came. His days of hiding his true self had ended. No one would ever use his sexuality as a way to blackmail him. He beamed at Sam, cupped his face and gave him a slow kiss on the lips.

Nate grinned then nudged Gordy. "Get a room, lover. Some of us don't appreciate your PDAs."

Gordy broke the kiss and winked at Nate. "Jealous?"

Nate laughed. "No. I'm good. Sam doesn't carry my preferred set of equipment."

Gordy started to respond, but Coach Torres headed it off. "This is heading toward locker room banter, which means we're finished here." He glanced at the two football players. "You two take the rest of the day off, but tomorrow morning you have a seven o'clock appointment with Coach Morris. You both need work, and next week we're playing Texas. You must be at the top of your game. Get out of here and let's put this behind us."

Gordy considered what he should do, but nothing came to mind. He ran his gaze over everyone and smiled. "Thanks. I thought... Anyway, thanks."

"Go. Get something to eat," Torres said.

Gordy followed his advice and soon the three of them were leaving from the sports complex. They rounded a corner and Gordy saw his entire family marching across the quad, and Rachel was leading the pack. He looked to Sam, who was again turning a nice shade of pink.

"I might have called your parents. Your dad said he would fix this mess if it meant putting his boot in every ass on campus until they understood there was nothing wrong with his son, either of them." He nodded toward Rachel. "As for Rachel? Well, she fought as hard as any of us to fix everything that had gone wrong."

"This should be interesting," Gordy said.

Chapter Twenty-Two

A brisk chill nipped at Sam's cheeks. The sun was rising in the Colorado Rockies and the May night had dropped below freezing. The frost on their tent was a good indicator of the colder temperature. An early morning breeze wound its way across the small meadow and set the aspen leaves dancing. Gordy had suggested they take a trip after graduation, and Sam had enjoyed the week of camping, hiking and general sightseeing. He'd never been to this part of Colorado, and it was a lot of fun, even if this morning the chill was making his good bits play the turtle game. A stronger breeze set the tent covering popping, and Sam burrowed for Gordy. A few seconds later, he'd wrapped around the man and was enjoying the heat radiating from him.

A deep growl came from the other side of their bed, and Gordy wrapped his thick arms around him. The heat, muscles and hair had him thinking about more than the gorgeous scenery. When Gordy ran his hands down Sam's torso, his body responded to the attention as it did each time Gordy got affectionate. Sam twisted and scooted until he lay on top of Gordy's naked body. He wriggled, ran his hands over Gordy's weeklong growth of beard then kissed him. They pressed their lips hard together until Sam became more demanding and plunged his tongue into Gordy's mouth. An instant later, Gordy challenged him and their tongues battled. Sam ached for more when they broke the kiss.

"Hot damn, you can wake me up like this every day of the week," Gordy said.

Sam ground against Gordy, loving their hard cocks slipping over each other. As pre-cum coated both of them, the slick sensations became even better. Sam gripped Gordy tightly as he humped his cock on Gordy, his balls hugging his body.

"You're so fucking sexy," Sam whispered into Gordy's ear. Gordy responded by running his hand down Sam's back then squeezing his ass. Sam gasped as Gordy sank his fingers into his clenched butt. He twisted lower, running his hands over Gordy's chest as he chewed a line down the side of his neck. The slightly salty flavor and the scent that was pure Gordy kept him ready for the next step.

"Scoot up here. I want to lick your dick."

"It's fucking cold!"

Gordy laughed and dove into the double sleeping bag. Sam chuckled as Gordy worked to reach his goal, and before long, Gordy's hot mouth surrounded Sam's throbbing cock. When Gordy dug under his foreskin, it had Sam trembling. He lost track of the things Gordy did as his impending orgasm built. When Gordy sucked one of his balls into his hot mouth, he grabbed his hair and yanked.

"Stop, stop or I'll come, and I'm not ready."

Gordy pressed his tongue along the underside of Sam's dick and ran it to the head before coming loose and kissing Sam hard. The smells covered Gordy's face. They exchanged passionate kisses until Sam gasped for air. When they stopped, Sam smirked. "Roll over. I want you on your back."

Gordy complied without a question, but his smile grew when Sam pulled out a small bottle of lube from his backpack. He tossed the bottle to Gordy and turned so his ass was within reach. Gordy went to work and dribbled a trail of the thick liquid until it ran down Sam's crack. With each pass of Gordy's fingers, Sam wanted more. Gordy teased at his opening and applied lube several times before he sank a finger deep inside. The burn as it opened was painful, and delightful. He spread his legs wider and moaned.

"Fuck. That's amazing," Sam said.

Sam gasped with pleasure as Gordy opened him. Soon he couldn't wait any longer and pressed Gordy to his back. His body ached as he crawled on top and ground his ass down. He lasted only a few seconds before needing more. He paused, grabbed Gordy's cock and pressed himself onto it. The thick shaft slipped inside, and Sam worked it deeper. His body accommodated the intruder and soon Gordy's bush ground against his skin. He paused for a moment, letting himself adjust.

Sam worked himself faster until he was riding Gordy without conscious thought. It felt amazing, and nothing else mattered. As he moved back and forth, his rigid cock swung, leaving a trail of pre-cum. Sam was aching for release, but he struggled to hold out until their roles could be reversed.

Gordy thrust into him and Sam leaned forward to caress his chest. As Gordy pounded harder, Sam grabbed his nipples and twisted them.

"Fuck! Yeah, harder."

Sam twisted and tugged at Gordy's big nipples as he pounded Sam. The thrusts became more erratic, his gasps more uncontrolled. Gordy was close. He buried himself inside until Sam trembled. Gordy grabbed his thighs, froze in position and shook. Sam's cock thickened, and he could sense as Gordy filled him with hot cum. As his climax dwindled, Sam ran his hands over Gordy. Once his breathing was closer to normal, Gordy grinned.

"That was amazing. What happened to being cold?"

"Get on your stomach and I'll show you how I'm keeping warm."

Without a word, Gordy rolled over, shaking his ass and grinning. Sam grabbed the bottle of lube that had fallen close by and coated Gordy's crack. He gathered gel with his fingers and eased two inside. Once they were buried, he waited a moment and fingered Gordy. A low sigh came from the big guy as Sam slipped in a third finger a minute later.

"Oh, man. That's so good."

Sam squirmed into position and pried Gordy's ass open. He leaned forward and sank himself deep inside. The tight heat set every nerve into a lustful interplay. He tried to give Gordy time to adjust, but he was too far gone to wait more than a few seconds. Waves of euphoria washed over Sam until he knew his time was coming. Sam thrust harder with each moment until he plummeted over the edge. He buried himself deeply and held onto Gordy as the first wave of ecstasy passed through him. His body convulsed with each release until the last of it passed with a sigh.

"Oh. My. God," Sam groaned.

Sam writhed with his cock still buried inside Gordy. His breath slowed from gasps, as Gordy seemed content to have Sam lay on top of him. But after a few minutes, Sam stirred.

"Cold?" Gordy asked.

"Maybe…"

Gordy shifted around in their bed until he had Sam spooned against him. From there, it was easy to pull the thick sleeping bag over them. Sam relished the heat and even more the strong scent of amazing sex. He trembled when Gordy leaned in close and kissed his neck.

"I love you. You're amazing," Gordy said.

Tears rolled down Sam's face as he turned and kissed Gordy. "I love you, too."

* * * *

The warm afternoon sun beamed over Sam's bare back as he worked to be certain their fire was out. This was their last day of vacation and it had been a wonderful week. The scenery was beautiful and the sex mind-blowing. Sam's auburn hair twisted in the breeze and the tufts of hair under each arm drew Gordy closer. He stood watching, realizing he loved this man more with each passing day.

Sam turned toward him and grinned. "Hey, handsome. The vacation is almost over. But it's been fun. I'm glad you came up with the idea."

Gordy shrugged, feeling his heart race as he tried to control himself. "It was a blast. Now we've got the rest of the summer to move to A&M. It'll be a big change for us."

Sam stood and dusted off his hands before he moved close enough to Gordy to give him a kiss. "It'll be fine. You've got a full-ride academic scholarship and a grad assistantship. I'm sure I can get a job at the computer help desk. They're always needing experienced people. So, that year of working IT at State will make the job thing easy."

"It'll be a long way from home, and who knows how they'll accept us. I might not be on the football team any more, but there are assholes everywhere."

"Why are you getting cold feet suddenly? We've talked about it. As long as I have you, things will be fine," Sam said.

Gordy motioned to the opposite side of the clearing. "What's that?"

Sam pulled on his shirt as he scanned the area. "I don't see anything. What'd you think it—" He'd turned back and found a shaking Gordy on one knee. Sam asked in a whisper, "What are you doing?"

"Be quiet. I'm already about to puke from nerves."

Sam nodded but reached over and wiped the tears from Gordy's cheeks. He stood without speaking while Gordy swallowed hard, looked up at Sam and grinned.

"When we first met, you thought I was a stupid jock and I thought you were a pompous jerk. We've been through a lot since then. Now we're off to new adventures, and I can't imagine doing them without you at my side. Samuel Doherty, I love you. Would you marry me and make me the happiest man alive?"

He looked up and tears streamed down Sam's face. He didn't look any calmer than Gordy, but he appeared happy. Gordy knelt there until the silence stretched too long and the sobs from Sam got louder. He started to panic.

"Well? You gonna marry me?" Then he realized he'd missed an important step. "Oh hell. I have rings, too." He opened his hand that held two titanium wedding bands. Sam laughed through his tears, took the smaller ring and slipped it on his finger before tugging Gordy to his feet.

"Yes. Yes! Of course, I'll marry you. You're my whole life." He took the other ring and threaded it onto Gordy's finger. After another minute had passed, Sam chuckled. "How long have you had the rings?"

Gordy grinned. "A few months. There's never been the perfect time to propose."

"Does your family know?"

"Not when I was going to pop the question, but I told them we were getting married."

"And?"

Gordy beamed. "We can have our ceremony at the ranch and my brother is our wedding planner."

"Oh crap. This will be one for the ages."

"Oh yeah. Ardmore may never recover," Gordy said with a grin.

"Then it'll be the perfect wedding."

More books from
Pride Publishing

Book three in the Dublin Virtues series

When everything changes, can renewal bring redemption?

Part of the Anthem Trilogy

An ocean of possibility. For love, revenge and murder.

THE SMELL OF
Camellias

BROKEN TO BE WHOLE...

REMMY
DUCHENE

Broken to be whole…

Book one in the Responsible Adult serial

Life isn't always responsible

About the Author

Jon Keys

Jon Keys' earliest memories revolve around books; with the first ones he can recall reading himself being "The Warlord of Mars" and anything with Tarzan. (The local library wasn't particularly up to date.) But as puberty set in, he started sneaking his mother's romance magazines and added the world of romance and erotica to his mix of science fiction, fantasy, Native American, westerns and comic books.

A voracious reader for almost half a century, Jon has only recently begun creating his own flights of fiction for the entertainment of others. Born in the Southwest and now living in the Midwest, Jon has worked as a ranch hand, teacher, computer tech, roughneck, designer, retail clerk, welder, artist, and, yes, pool boy; with interests ranging from kayaking and hunting to painting and cooking, he draws from a wide range of life experiences to create written works that draw the reader in and wrap them in a good story.

Jon Keys loves to hear from readers. You can find contact information, website details and an author profile page at https://www.pride-publishing.com/